Phil Bambridge

Nathan Filer is a writer and lecturer in creative writing at Bath Spa University. A registered mental health nurse, he has worked as a researcher in the academic unit of psychiatry at the University of Bristol and on in-patient wards. He is also a performance poet whose work has been broadcast on television and radio.

The Shock of the Fall is Nathan's first novel and the recipient of the 2013 Costa Book of the Year and the 2014 Betty Trask Prize.

Praise for *The Shock of the Fall*

"I have become an evangelist for *The Shock of the Fall*. It won me heart and soul with its crazy, wild, fine voice, its bravura, its ambition, its harrowing corners, and the dense, rich, tiny core of love at its glowing, radiant center. In Matthew's admittedly hard world, the tiniest kindnesses echo and amplify, returning to him larger and louder, until they each become glorious—huge bursts of such grace and truth that more than once, I had to stop reading and weep at the sheer hope-soaked beauty of it. I loved this book cover to cover and word by word; I want to give it to everyone I care for, and I want to keep it for myself to reread over and over." —Joshilyn Jackson, *New York Times* bestselling author of *A Grown-Up Kind of Pretty*

"Skillfully done books transcend age categories. This helps explain the success of such books as *The Fault in Our Stars* and *The Perks of Being a Wallflower*, and the endurance of *The Catcher in the Rye*. [*The Shock of the Fall*] is indeed skillfully done, with drama enough to lure teen readers and sophistication enough to keep adults entranced." —*The Plain Dealer*

"A page-turner, tender and tragic, told in a vulnerable voice that steps in and out of madness. Vivid and haunting, I keep replaying this story in my mind, reliving it, long after having read the final page." —Lisa Genova, *New York Times* bestselling author of *Still Alice* and *Love Anthony*

"Original and affecting. Filer's ability to capture Matthew's voice shows a special talent."

—Heidi W. Durrow, *New York Times* bestselling author of *The Girl Who Fell from the Sky*

"It should prove catnip to book group participants (especially those who loved Mark Haddon's *The Curious Incident of the Dog in the Night-Time*) and will appeal to anyone looking for a serious (but not ponderous) story that's impossible to put down." — *Library Journal* (starred review)

"Quietly horrifying and surprisingly beautiful: a portrait of family love. Unsentimental, frank, and strange, Filer's narrator is the most likable nut since Kesey's Chief. I can't stop talking about this book. Looking for a fantastic read, a few laughs, and a good cry? You've found it. *The Shock of the Fall* is a fresh, smart book with a big, daft heart."

—Lydia Netzer, author of *How to Tell Toledo from the Night Sky*

"*The Shock of the Fall* is a stunning novel. Ambitious and exquisitely realized, it's by turns shocking, harrowing, and heartrending. The writing is so accomplished it's hard to believe it's a debut—it's clearly the work of a major new talent."

—S. J. Watson, *New York Times* bestselling author of *Before I Go to Sleep*

THE SHOCK OF THE FALL

Nathan Filer

St. Martin's Griffin New York

THE SHOCK OF THE FALL. Copyright © 2013 by Nathan Filer. All rights reserved. Printed in the United States of America. For information address St. Martin's Press, 175 Fifth Avenue, New York, N.Y. 10010.

Illustrations by Charlotte Farmer

www.stmartins.com

The Library of Congress has cataloged the hardcover edition as follows:

Filer, Nathan.
  [Shock of the Fall]
  Where the Moon Isn't : a novel / Nathan Filer.—1st U.S. Edition.
    p. cm.
  ISBN 978-1-250-02698-9 (hardcover)
  ISBN 978-1-250-02699-6 (e-book)
  1. Schizophrenia—Patients—Fiction.   2. Life change events—
Fiction.   3. Psychological fiction.   I. Title.
  PR6106.I44S56 2013
  823'.92—dc23

                                                    2013025459

ISBN 978-1-250-02813-6 (trade paperback)

St. Martin's Griffin books may be purchased for educational, business, or promotional use. For information on bulk purchases, please contact the Macmillan Corporate and Premium Sales Department at 1-800-221-7945, extension 5442, or write to specialmarkets@macmillan.com.

First published in Great Britain under the title
The Shock of the Fall by HarperCollins*Publishers*

Previously published as *Where the Moon Isn't*

First St. Martin's Griffin Edition: January 2015

10 9 8 7 6 5 4 3 2

For Emily

The Shock of the Fall

the girl and her doll

I should say that I am not a nice person. Sometimes I try to be, but often I'm not. So when it was my turn to cover my eyes and count to a hundred – I cheated.

I stood at the spot where you had to stand when it was your turn to count, which was beside the recycling bins, next to the shop selling disposable barbecues and spare tent pegs. And near to there is a small patch of overgrown grass, tucked away behind a water tap.

Except I don't remember standing there. Not really. You don't always remember the details like that, do you? You don't remember if you were beside the recycling bins, or further up the path near to the shower blocks, and whether actually the water tap is up there?

I can't now hear the manic cry of seagulls, or taste the salt in the air. I don't feel the heat of the afternoon sun making me sweat beneath a clean white dressing on my knee, or the itching of suncream in the cracks of my scabs. I can't make myself relive the vague sensation of having been abandoned. And neither – for what it's worth – do I actually remember deciding to cheat, and open my eyes.

She looked about my age, with red hair and a face flecked in hundreds of freckles. Her cream dress was dusty around the hem from kneeling on the ground, and clutched to her chest was a small cloth doll, with a smudged pink face, brown woollen hair, and eyes made of shining black buttons.

The first thing she did was place her doll beside her, resting it ever so gently on the long grass. It looked comfortable, with its arms flopped to the sides and its head propped up a little. I thought it looked comfortable anyway.

We were so close I could hear the scratching and scraping, as she began to break up the dry ground with a stick. She didn't notice me though, even when she threw the stick away and it nearly landed on my toes, all exposed in my stupid plastic flip-flops. I would have been wearing my trainers but you know what my mum's like. Trainers, on a lovely day like today. Surely not. She's like that.

A wasp buzzed around my head, and usually that would be enough to get me flapping around all over the place, except I didn't let myself. I stayed totally still, not wanting to disturb the little girl, or not wanting her to know I was there. She was digging with her fingers now, pulling up the dry earth with her bare hands, until the hole was deep enough. Then she rubbed the dirt from her fingers as best she could, picked up her doll again, and kissed it twice.

That is the part I can still see most clearly – those two kisses, one on its forehead, one on the cheek.

I forgot to say, but the doll wore a coat. It was bright yellow, with a black plastic buckle at the front. This is important because the next thing she did was undo the buckle, and take this coat off. She did this very quickly, and stuffed it down the front of her dress.

Sometimes – times like now – when I think of those two kisses, it is as though I can actually feel them.

One on the forehead.

One on the cheek.

What happened next is less clear in my mind because it has merged into so many other memories, been played out in so many other ways that I can't separate the real from the imagined, or even be sure there is a difference. So I don't know exactly when she started to cry, or if she was crying already. And I don't know if she hesitated before throwing the last handful of dirt. But I do know by the time the doll was covered, and the earth patted down, she was bent over, clutching the yellow coat to her chest, and weeping.

When you're a nine-year-old boy, it's no easy thing to comfort a girl. Especially if you don't know her, or even what the matter is.

I gave it my best shot.

Intending to rest my arm lightly across her shoulders – the way Dad did to Mum when we took family walks – I shuffled forward, where in a moment of indecision I couldn't commit either to kneeling beside her or staying standing. I hovered awkwardly between the two, then overbalanced, toppling in slow motion, so the first this weeping girl was aware of me, was the entire weight of my body, gently pushing her face into a freshly dug grave. I still don't know what I should have said to make things better, and I've thought about this a lot. But lying beside her with the tips of our noses nearly touching, I tried, 'I'm Matthew. What's your name?'

She didn't answer straight away. She tilted her head to get a better look at me, and as she did that I felt a single strand of her long hair slip quickly across the side of my tongue, leaving my mouth at the corner. 'I'm Annabelle,' she said.

Her name was Annabelle.

The girl with the red hair and a face flecked in hundreds of freckles is called Annabelle. Try and remember that if you can. Hold onto it through everything else that happens in life, through all the things that might make you want to forget – keep it safe somewhere.

I stood up. The dressing on my knee was now a dirty brown. I started to say we were playing hide-and-seek, that she could play too if she wanted. But she interrupted. She spoke calmly, not sounding angry or upset. And what she said was, 'You're not welcome here any more, Matthew.'

'What?'

She didn't look at me, she drew herself onto her hands and knees and focused on the small pile of loose earth – patting it neat again, making it perfect. 'This is my daddy's caravan park. I live here, and you're not welcome. Go home.'

'But—'

'Get lost!'

She was upright in an instant, moving towards me with her chest puffed out, like a small animal trying to look bigger. She said it again, 'Get lost, I told you. You're not welcome.'

A seagull laughed mockingly, and Annabelle shouted, 'You've ruined everything.'

It was too late to explain. By the time I reached the footpath, she was kneeling on the ground again, the little yellow doll's coat held to her face.

The other children were shouting out, calling to be found. But I didn't look for them. Past the shower blocks, past the shop, cutting through the park – I ran as fast as I could, my flip-flops slapping on the hot tarmac. I didn't let myself stop, I didn't even let myself slow down until I was close enough to our caravan to see Mum sitting out on the deckchair. She was wearing her straw sun hat, and looking out to the sea. She smiled and waved at me, but I knew I was still in her bad books. We'd sort of fallen out a few days before. It's stupid because it was only really me who got hurt, and the scabs were nearly healed now, but my parents sometimes find it hard to let stuff go.

Mum in particular, she holds grudges.

I guess I do too.

I'll tell you what happened because it will be a good way to introduce my brother. His name's Simon. I think you're going to like him. I really do. But in a couple of pages he'll be dead. And he was never the same after that.

When we arrived at Ocean Cove Holiday Park – bored from the journey, and desperate to explore – we were told it was okay for us to go anywhere in the site, but were forbidden from going to the beach by ourselves because of how steep and uneven the path is. And because you have to go onto the main road for a bit to get to the top of it. Our parents were the kind to worry about that sort of thing – about steep paths and main roads. I decided to go to the beach anyway. I often did things that I wasn't allowed to do, and my brother would follow. If I hadn't decided to name this part of my story **the girl and her doll** then I could have named it, **the shock of the fall and the blood on my knee** because that was important too.

There was the shock of the fall and the blood on my knee. I've never been good with pain. This is something I hate about myself. I'm a total wimp. By the time Simon caught up with me, at the twist in the path where exposed roots snare unsuspecting ankles – I was wailing like a baby.

He looked so worried it was almost funny. He had a big round face, which was forever smiling and made me think of the moon. But suddenly he looked so fucking worried.

This is what Simon did. He collected me in his arms and carried me step-by-step back up the cliff path, and the quarter of a mile or so to our caravan. He did that for me.

I think a couple of adults tried to help, but the thing you need to know about Simon is that he was a bit different from most people you might meet. He went to a special school where they were taught basic stuff like not talking to strangers, so whenever he felt unsure of himself or panicked, he would retreat to these lessons to feel safe. That's the way he worked.

He carried me all by himself. But he wasn't strong. This was a symptom of his disorder, a weakness of the muscles. It has a name that I can't think of now, but I'll look it up if I get the chance. It meant that the walk half killed him. So when we got back to the caravan he had to spend the rest of the day in bed.

Here are the three things I remember most clearly from when Simon carried me:

1/ The way my chin banged against his shoulder as he walked. I worried that I was hurting him, but I was too wrapped up in my own pain to say anything.

2/ So I kissed his shoulder better, in the way that when you're little you believe this actually works. I don't think he noticed though, because my chin was banging against him with every step, and when I kissed him, my teeth banged instead, which, if anything, probably hurt more.

3/ Shhh, shhh. It'll be okay. That's what he said as he placed me down outside our caravan, before running in to get Mum. I might not have been clear enough – Simon really wasn't strong. Carrying me like that was the hardest thing he'd ever done, but still he tried to reassure me. Shhh, shhh. It'll be okay. He sounded so grown-up, so gentle and certain. For the first time in my life it truly felt like I had a big brother. In the few short seconds whilst I waited for Mum to come out, as I cradled my knee, stared at the dirt and grit in the skin, convinced myself I could see the bone, in those few short seconds – I felt totally safe.

Mum cleaned and dressed the wound, then she shouted at me for putting Simon in such a horrible position. Dad shouted at me too. At one point they were both shouting together, so that I wasn't even sure who to look at. This was the way it worked. Even though my brother was three years older, it was always me who was responsible for everything. I often resented him for that. But not this time. This time he was my hero.

So that's my story to introduce Simon. And it's also the reason I was still in Mum's bad books as I arrived, breathless, at our caravan, trying to make sense of what had happened with the small girl and her cloth doll.

'Sweetheart, you're ashen.'

She's always calling me ashen, my mum. These days she calls me it all the time. But I forgot she said it way back then too. I completely forgot that she's always called me ashen.

'I'm sorry about the other day, Mum.' And I was sorry. I'd been thinking about it a lot. About how Simon had to carry me, and how worried he had looked.

'It's okay, sweetheart. We're on holiday. Try and enjoy yourself. Your dad went down to the beach with Simon, they've taken the kite. Shall we join them?'

'I think I'm going to stay in for a bit. It's hot out. I think I'm going to watch some telly.'

'On a lovely day like today? Honestly, Matthew. What are we going to do with you?'

She sort of asked that in a friendly way, as though she didn't really feel a need to do anything with me. She could be nice like that. She could definitely be nice like that.

'I don't know Mum. Sorry about the other day. Sorry about everything.'

'It's forgotten sweetheart, really.'

'Promise?'

'I promise. Let's go and fly that kite, shall we?'

'I don't feel like it.'

'You're not watching telly, Matt.'

'I'm in the middle of a game of hide-and-seek.'

'You're hiding?'

'No. I'm seeking. I should do that really.'

But the other children had got bored of waiting to be found, and had broken off into smaller groups, and other games. I didn't feel like playing anyway. So I wandered around for a bit, and I found myself back at the place where the girl had been. Only she wasn't there any more. There was just the small mound of earth, now carefully decorated with a few picked buttercups and daisies, and – to mark the spot – two sticks, placed neatly in a cross.

I felt very sad. And I feel a bit sad even thinking about it. Anyway, I have to go. Jeanette from Art Group's doing her nervous bird impression; fluttering around at the top of the corridor, trying to catch my attention.

That paper-mache won't make itself.

I have to go.

family portraits

The next thing I knew Mum was turning up the volume of the radio, so I wouldn't hear her crying.

It was stupid. I could hear her. I was sitting right behind her in the car and she was crying really loudly. So was Dad for that matter. He was crying and driving at the same time. I honestly didn't know if I was crying too, but I figured that I probably was. It seemed like I should be anyway. So I touched my cheeks, but it turned out they were dry. I wasn't crying at all.

This is what people mean when they talk about being numb, isn't it? I was too numb to cry, you sometimes hear people say on the TV. Like on daytime chat shows or whatever. I couldn't even feel anything, they explain. I was just completely numb. And the people in the audience nod sympathetically, like they've all been there, they all know exactly how this feels. I reckon it was like that, but at the time I felt very guilty about it. I buried my head in my hands, so that if Mum or Dad turned around, they would think I was crying with them.

They didn't turn around. I never felt the reassuring squeeze

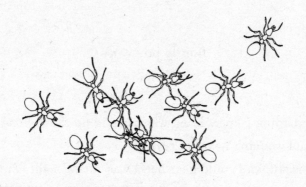

of a hand on my leg, they never said it would be okay. Nobody whispered, Shhh, shhh.

I knew then – I was totally alone.

It was a strange thing to find out that way.

On the radio the DJ was introducing some new song in this really chipper voice, like it was the best song ever recorded and it made his life complete to be able to introduce it. But none of this made any sense to me. I couldn't understand why the DJ was so happy when something so terrible had happened. That was my first proper thought. It was the thing that I remember thinking as I sort of woke up. And this is the best way that I can describe it, even though I hadn't really been asleep.

Memories were falling away, like a dream when we first open our eyes. It was a lot like that. I could only make out the edges – night-time, running, the police were there somewhere.

And Simon was dead.

My brother was dead.

I couldn't hold onto any of it though. I wouldn't get to hold it again for a very long time.

I can't talk about it yet either. I have one chance to get this right. I need to be careful. To unfold everything neatly, so that I know how to fold it away again if it all gets too much. And everyone knows, the best way to fold something neatly is to follow the folds that are already there.

*

My grandmother (Mum's mum, the one we call Nanny Noo) reads books by Danielle Steel and Catherine Cookson, and whenever she gets a new one the first thing she does is flip straight to the back to read the last page.

She always does that.

I went to stay with her for a bit. Just for the first week or so. It was a very sad week, and probably the most lonely of my life. I don't think it is even possible to feel more lonely, even if you didn't have your granddad and your Nanny Noo to keep you company.

You've probably never met my granddad, but if you have then you will know that he is a keen gardener. Only he doesn't have a garden. That's kind of funny if you think about it. But it isn't that funny because he rents a small allotment a short drive from their flat, where he is able to grow vegetables and a few herbs like rosemary and some others that I always forget.

That week we spent ages there. Sometimes I would help with the weeding, or sometimes I would sit at the edge of his patch of allotment and play Donkey Kong on my Game Boy Color, so long as I kept the volume turned down. Mostly though, I would just wander about lifting stones to look at insects. I liked ants the best. Simon and I always used to look for ants' nests in our own garden. He thought they were brilliant, and he pleaded with our mum to let him have an Ant Farm in his room. He usually got his way. But not that time.

Granddad helped me lift the bigger paving slabs so I could see the nests. The moment a slab was lifted the ants would go mental, scurrying around passing secret messages to each other and carrying their tiny white and yellow eggs underground to safety.

Within a couple of minutes the surface would be completely deserted, except for maybe a few woodlice wandering clumsily through to see what all the fuss was about. Occasionally I'd poke a twig down one of the little holes, and in an instant a dozen soldier ants would be back out on the offensive, prepared to give their lives for the colony. Not that I ever hurt them. I only wanted to watch.

After Granddad had finished weeding or pulling up vegetables or planting new ones, we'd carefully place back the slab and head home for our tea. I don't remember us ever talking. I know we must have done. But what words we shared have escaped from my memory completely, like ants down a hole.

Nanny Noo made nice food. She is one of those people who tries to feed you the moment you walk through the door, and doesn't stop trying to feed you until the moment you leave. She might even make you a quick ham sandwich for your journey.

It is a nice way to be. I think people who are generous with food have a goodness about them. But that week or so that I stayed with them was very difficult because I had no appetite. I felt sick a lot of the time, and once or twice I actually was sick. This was difficult for Nanny Noo too, because if she couldn't solve a problem through the stomach – like with a bowl of soup or a roasted chicken or a slice of Battenberg – she felt out of her depth. One time I spied her standing in the kitchen, hunched over the untouched dishes and sobbing.

Bedtimes were hardest. I was staying in the spare room, which never gets properly dark because there is a street lamp outside the window and the curtains are thin. I would lie awake each night for ages and ages, staring through the gloom, wishing that I could just go home, and wondering if I ever would.

'Can I sleep in here tonight, Nanny?'

She didn't stir, so I walked in slowly and lifted the corner of her quilt. Nanny Noo has one of those electric blankets on account of her cold bones. It was a warm night though, so it wasn't plugged in, and next thing I knew I was letting out a quiet yelp as my bare foot pressed down onto the upturned plug.

'Sweetheart?'

'Are you awake, Nanny?'

'Shhh, you'll wake up Granddad.'

She lifted the quilt and I climbed in beside her, 'I stood on the plug,' I said. 'I hurt my foot a bit.'

I could feel the warmth of Nanny's breath against my ear. I could hear Granddad's rhythmic snoring.

'I can't remember anything,' I said at last. 'I don't know what happened. I don't know what I did.'

At least I wanted to say that. It was all I could think about, and I desperately wanted to say it, but that isn't the same thing. I could feel Nanny's breath against my ear. 'You stood on the plug, my poor angel. You hurt your foot.'

When I went home it was just Mum and Dad and me. On our first evening together the three of us sank onto the big green couch, which is how it always was because Simon preferred to sit cross-legged on the carpet – his face right up close to the television.

That was sort of our family portrait. It's not the kind of thing you think you would miss. Maybe you don't even notice it all those thousands of times, sitting between your mum and dad on the big green couch with your big brother on the carpet getting in the way of the telly. Maybe you don't even notice that.

But you notice it when he isn't there any more. You notice so many of the places where he isn't, and you hear so many of the things he doesn't say.

I do.

I hear them all the time.

Mum switched on the television for the start of EastEnders. This was like a ritual. We even videoed it if we weren't going to be home. It was funny because Simon had a huge crush on Bianca. We all used to tease him about it and tell him that Ricky would beat him up. It was only for fun. He used to laugh out loud, rolling about on the carpet. He had the sort of laugh people call infectious. Whenever he laughed it made everything that bit better.

I don't know if you watch EastEnders, or even if you do, I don't suppose you'll remember an episode from so long ago. But this one stayed with me. I remember sitting on the couch and watching as all the lies and deceit about Bianca sleeping with her mum's boyfriend and a whole load of other stuff finally came to its bitter conclusion. This was the episode when Bianca left Walford.

We didn't speak for a long time after that. We didn't even move. Other programmes started and ended well into the night. This was our new family portrait – the three of us, sitting side by side, staring at the space where Simon used to be.

PLEASE STOP READING OVER MY SHOULDER

She keeps reading over my shoulder. It is hard enough to concentrate in this place without people reading over your shoulder.

I had to put that in big letters to drive the message home. It worked, but now I feel bad about it. It was the student social worker who was looking over my shoulder, the young one with the minty breath and big gold earrings. She's really nice.

Anyway, now she's skipped away down the corridor, acting bright and breezy. But I know that I've embarrassed her because people only skip like that, and act all bright and breezy, when they're embarrassed. We don't need to skip when we're not embarrassed – we can just walk.

It's good to be able to use this computer though. I had a teaching session on it with the occupational therapist. His name's Steve, and I don't suppose I'll mention him again. But he was satisfied I knew not to try to eat the keyboard, or whatever it is they worry about. So he said it's okay for me to use it for my writing. Except he still didn't give me a password, so I have to ask each time, and we only get forty minutes. It's like that here, forty minutes for this, and ten minutes for that. But I am sorry about embarrassing that student social worker. I really am. I hate stuff like that.

kicking and wailing

I had no right to attend my brother's funeral. But I did attend. I wore a white polyester shirt that itched like mad around the collar, and a black clip-on tie. The church echoed whenever anyone coughed. And afterwards there were scones with cream and jam. And that is all I can remember.

But now I should slow down a bit. I tend to rush when I'm nervous. I do it when I'm speaking too, which is weird because you tend to think it's just those small tightly wound men who speak quickly. I'm about six feet tall and might even still be growing. I'm nineteen, so maybe not. I'm definitely growing outwards though. I'm way fatter than I should be. We can blame the medication for that – it's a common side effect.

Anyway, I speak too quickly. I rush through words I find uncomfortable, and I'm doing that now.

I need to slow down because I want to explain how my world slowed down. I also need to talk about how life has a shape and a size, and how it can be made to fit into something small – like a house.

But the first thing I want to say is how quiet everything got. That was the first thing I noticed. It was as though somebody had come along and turned the volume to just above mute, and now everyone felt a need to talk in whispers. Not just Mum and Dad, but people who came to visit us too – like something terrible was asleep in the corner of the room and nobody dared be the one to wake it.

I'm talking about relatives here, people like my aunties and grandparents. My parents were never the sort to have loads of friends. I had a few. But they were at school. That was the other thing that happened. I think I might be rushing again, but I'll just tell you quickly about how I stopped going to school, because it's important, and because it is an actual thing that happened. Most of life isn't anything. Most of life is just the passing of time, and we're even asleep for a fair chunk of that.

When I'm heavily medicated I sleep for up to eighteen hours a day. During these times I am far more interested in my dreams than in reality, because they take up so much more of my time. If I'm having nice dreams, I consider life to be pretty good. When the medication isn't working properly – or if I decide not to take it – I spend more time awake. But then my dreams have a way of following me.

It's like we each have a wall that separates our dreams from reality, but mine has cracks in it. The dreams can wriggle and squeeze their way through, until it's hard to know the difference.

Sometimes

the

wall

        breaks

             completely.

It's then

       that

   the

     nightmares come.

But now I'm getting distracted.

I'm forever getting distracted. I need to concentrate, because there is a lot I want to write about – like this stuff about my school. Summer was over. September was edging to a close, and I still hadn't been back to the classroom. So a decision had to be made.

The headmaster phoned and I listened to Mum's half of the conversation from **the watching stair**. It wasn't much of a conversation though. Basically she just said thank you a load of times. Then she called me to the telephone for my turn.

It was weird, because I never really talked to my headmaster at school. I mean, you really only talk to your teachers. I can't say for sure that I had ever once spoken to my headmaster, and now here he was on the end of the telephone saying, 'Hello Matthew, it's Mr Rogers.'

'Hello sir,' I managed. My voice sounded very small all of a sudden. I waited for him to say something else, and Mum squeezed my shoulder.

'I've just been speaking with your mum, but I wanted to talk to you too. Is that okay?'

'Yes.'

'I know this is a very difficult and sad time for you. I can only imagine how hard it must be.'

I didn't say anything because I didn't know what there was to say, so there was a really long silence. Then I started to agree that it was hard, but Mr Rogers started talking again at the same time, repeating that it was sad. So then we both stopped to let the other one talk, and neither of us said anything. Mum rubbed at the top of my back. I've never been any good on the phone.

'Matthew, I won't keep you because I know this is hard. But I wanted to tell you that everyone is thinking of you, that we miss you. And however long this takes, however long you need, you'll be welcomed back warmly. So you mustn't be afraid.'

That was a strange thing for him to say because I don't think I was afraid until then. I felt a lot of things – a lot that I didn't properly understand – but not afraid. Except when he said that, I suddenly was. So I just said thank you a few times too, and Mum gave me a weak smile that didn't reach her eyes. 'Do you want to speak to my mum again?'

'I think we're done for now,' Mr Rogers said. 'I'd just wanted to say a few words to you. We'll see you soon, okay?'

I let the phone drop into its cradle with a loud *clunk*.

He didn't see me soon. I didn't go back to school for a long time, and never to that school. I don't know how these decisions were made. That's the thing when you are nine years old; you don't really get told anything. Like if you are taken out of school nobody has to tell you why. People don't have to tell you anything. I think, though, most of the things we do, are driven by fear. I think my mum was very frightened of losing me. I think that is what it was. But I don't want to put thoughts in your head.

If you're a parent you can stop your children going to school, and sit them at the kitchen table with a workbook instead. Just write a letter to the head, and that is it. You don't even need to be a teacher, although Mum was. Sort of. I should tell you about my mum, because you probably have never met her.

She is thin and pale, with cold hands. She has a broad chin that she is very self-conscious about. She sniffs the milk before she drinks it. She loves me. And she is mad. That will do for now.

I say that she was sort of a teacher because once upon a time she was going to be. This was when she was trying to get pregnant, but there were some complications and the doctors said that she might not be able to conceive. I know this stuff, without any recollection of being told it. I think she decided to become a teacher to give her life a meaning, or to distract her. I don't suppose there is much difference.

So she enrolled at university and did the course. Then she got pregnant with Simon, and her meaning came kicking and wailing the regular way.

But she got to be my teacher. Each and every weekday, after Dad had set off for work, our school day would begin. First we would clear the breakfast table together, stacking plates and bowls by the sink for Mum to wash whilst I made a start on the pile of Key Stage exercise books. I was a clever child back then. I think that took Mum by surprise.

When Simon was alive he could be a bit of a sponge, soaking up the attention. He didn't mean to or anything, but that is what special needs do – they demand more of the things around them. I seemed to go unnoticed. But sitting at the kitchen table, Mum did notice me. It might have been easier for her if I had been stupid. I only just thought that now as I wrote it, but it might be true. There were these tests at the end of each chapter of the Key Stage Science, Maths and French workbooks, and whenever I got everything right she would go quiet for ages. But if I only got nearly everything right, she would be encouraging, and gently talk me through my mistakes. That was weird. So I started making mistakes on purpose.

We never went out, and we never talked about anything except school work. That was strange too, because it wasn't as if Mum acted like a teacher. Sometimes she would kiss me on the forehead or stroke my hair or whatever. But we just didn't talk about any-thing except what was in the books. And that is exactly how the days unfolded for a long time, though I couldn't tell you exactly how long in terms of weeks or months. It merged into one extended moment, with me sitting at the kitchen table doing my tests, and Mum talking me through my deliberate mistakes.

That is what I mean by my world slowing down, but it is hard to explain because it only takes a couple of pages to say how it was day after day. But it is the day-after-day that takes so long.

When my work was done I would watch cartoons or play some Nintendo. Or sometimes I would go upstairs and gently press my ear against Simon's bedroom door, listening. Sometimes I would kill a bit of time doing that. We never talked about that either. Mum would make tea, and we would wait for my dad to get home. I should tell you about my dad, because you probably have never met him.

He is tall and broad, and stoops a little. He wears a leather jacket because he used to ride a motorbike. He calls me mon ami. And he loves me. That will do for now.

I said my mother is mad. I said that. But you might not see it. I mean, you might not think that anything I've told you proves she is mad. But there are different kinds of madness. Some madness doesn't act mad to begin with, sometimes it will knock politely at the door, and when you let it in, it'll simply sit in the corner without a fuss – and grow. Then one day, maybe many months after your decision to take your son out of school and isolate him in a house for reasons that got lost in your grief, one day that madness will stir in the chair, and it will say to him, 'You look pale.'

'What?'

'You look pale. You don't look well at all sweetheart. Are you feeling okay?'

'I'm fine, I think. I have a bit of a sore throat.'

'Let me feel you.' She put the back of her hand against my forehead. 'Oh, darling. You feel hot. You're burning up.'

'Really? I feel okay.'

'You've been looking pale for a few days now. I don't think you get enough sunshine.'

'We never go out!' I said that angrily. I didn't mean to, but that's the way it came out. It wasn't fair of me either because we did go out sometimes. I wasn't a prisoner or anything.

We didn't go out much, though. And never without Dad taking us. I suppose that's what I mean by saying how life can shrink into a house. I suppose I'm just ungrateful. Mum must have thought so, because she suddenly looked at me like I'd spat on her or something. But then she said very sweetly, 'Shall we go for a walk? We could pop in to see Dr Marlow, he can look at your throat.'

It wasn't cold, but she took my orange winter coat from the hook, and she zipped it right to the top with the hood pulled up. Then we stepped outside.

To get to the local GP surgery from our house, you had to walk past my school. Or rather, what used to be my school. Mum held my hand as we crossed the main road, and as we rounded the corner I could hear distant shouts and laughter drifting over from the playground. I must have resisted. I don't remember doing so on purpose, but I must have done because as we got closer Mum's grip on me tightened, taking hold of my wrist and pulling me along.

'Let's go back, Mum.'

We didn't go back. We walked right up to the school, and along the whole length of the fence so that I was practically being dragged, with my stupid hood right over my eyes.

'Is that you, Matthew? Hello Mrs Homes. Hello Matthew.'

I can't think of her name now. Gemma, or something. It doesn't matter anyway.

'Hey, it's Matthew!'

The thing is, I was even popular. The group of children who gathered at the fence did so because they liked me. They were my classmates and would have been shaken up by what had happened, and my sudden exit from their lives. But I didn't talk to them. I can't explain it. I looked straight ahead, hiding behind my hood, whilst Mum said, 'Matthew isn't very well today. Go back and play.'

Dr Marlow asked me to open wide. He looked inside my mouth, breathing his warm breath into me, smelling of coffee. There was nothing wrong with my throat that a few lozenges and some Lemsip couldn't fix. He said I should get some rest. So that was that. Only it wasn't.

It was just the start.

hypotonia *n.* a state of reduced tension in muscle.

There was the shock of the fall and the blood on my knee, and Simon carried me all the way back to the caravan, all by himself, without any help from anyone, even though it half killed him, but he did it anyway, he did it for me, because he loved me.

I already told you that.

And then I said there is a proper word for weak muscles, that I would look it up if I got the chance. And possibly you forgot all about it. But I didn't. I didn't forget.

There is a Nursing Dictionary kept in the office at the top of the back staircase, and I could see it there on the table. I could see it when I went to the office to ask if I could go on the computer for a while to do my writing.

It was really funny though, because the girl I asked (the young one with the minty breath and big gold earrings, who is forever trying to read over my shoulder), she just kind of froze. She was the only person in the office, and she totally froze, as if the Nursing Dictionary contains all these secrets that patients aren't allowed to know. Seriously, she couldn't even open her mouth.

Then a really funny thing happened. Do you remember Steve? I only mentioned him that once. He was the one who gave me the teaching session on this computer. I said that I probably wouldn't mention him again. Well, he came into the office next, and the girl turned to him and asked, really hesitantly, whether or not patients could look in the dictionary? That is how she said it too. She said 'Um, um, is it appropriate for patients to borrow the dictionary Steven?'

And you'll never guess what he did. He stepped past her, and in one move he threw the dictionary back through the air like a rugby pass, right into my hands. And at the same time he said, 'What ya askin' me for?' He said it just like that. He said, 'What ya askin' me for?'

Then he turned to me and winked. But it wasn't even a quiet wink, because he made a little clicking noise with his tongue as if to say, you and me kiddo, we're in this together.

Do you know what I mean? I don't know if I am explaining it very well. But you can see why it's funny. It's funny because the girl didn't know whether or not I could even look in the diction-ary. And then it was doubly funny because Steve made her look really stupid, by being all casual about it.

But the really funny thing. The thing that makes me laugh out loud. The really funny thing is that Steve made that little click-ing noise with his tongue, and winked at me, as if to show that he was on my side or something. Except you're not on my side, are you Steve? Because if you were on my side you just would have handed me the dictionary like a grown-up. Because if you make a

30

big fucking gesture of it Steve, then it becomes a big fucking deal. But that is what these people do – the Steves of this world – they all try and make something out of nothing. And they all do it for themselves.

Simon had hypotonia. He also had microgenia, macroglossia, epicanthic folds, an atrial septal defect, and a beautiful smiling face that looked like the moon. I hate this fucking place.

spoon fed

Mum pulled open the quilt at the entrance and peered inside, 'I've forgotten the password again.'

'You can't come in then.'

'Will you tell me it one more time?'

'Nope.' I pulled the quilt back against the radiator, gripping it tightly with my fist.

'Bully.'

'I'm not a bully, I've told you once already.'

'Super Mario?'

'Close.'

'Hmm. What's his girlfriend called?'

'Princess Peach.'

'Ah, yes. That's not it either, is it?'

'Uh-uh. Actually, she isn't Princess Peach in this game. And you're getting warmer. Sort of.'

'Cryptic clues, eh?'

'What does cryptic mean?'

'It means if you don't tell me the password I'll cry.'

I opened a small gap and watched as she made her pretend sad face, with bottom lip trembling. It was hard not to laugh.

'Oh, charming. Here I am, pouring my heart out, and my own son and heir is smirking at me.'

'I'm not smirking.'

'What's this then?' Her arm crept in, through a gap I hadn't noticed. She did that thing when you make a bird's beak with your hand, pecking up my arm until she found my face. She propped up the corners of my mouth. 'Ah-ha. I knew it!'

It's good being a bit ill when you're a kid, isn't it?

It's better if you go to a proper school, because then when you stay home for the day it's a treat. If you have your lessons at home anyway, there isn't anywhere to go. Unless you're allowed to build your own den.

'Okay,' I said. 'I'll give you a clue.'

'Go on then.'

'I'm playing it right … now.'

I let the entrance fall open and quickly picked up my Game Boy Color. Mum tilted her head, squinting at the cartridge. 'Donkey Kong!'

'You may enter.'

It was really just the space between the back of the couch and the wall, but I stretched a quilt over the top, tucking it behind the radiator. It was nice to hide away in there, playing games or watching TV through the gap beside the curtains.

Mum crouched on all fours and crawled inside. 'Show me how to play it then.'

'Really?'

'What, you don't think mummies can?'

There wasn't much room, but that made it better in a way. It was cosy. 'Hold it like that, with your thumbs on the buttons. See him at the bottom?'

'Uh-huh.'

'He's Mario. You need to make him climb to the top, without the barrels hitting you.'

'What's at the top?'

'His girlfriend.'

'Not the princess?'

'She's in other games. It's started, you need to concentrate—'

When the first barrel hit her, she said it wasn't fair because she was about to get good.

'It's still your go. You have more than one life. Shall I tell you when you need to jump?'

She didn't answer.

'Mum, shall I tell you when to jump?'

She kissed me on the cheek.

'Yes please.'

I'm not a mind-reader. I can't tell you what my mum was thinking. Sometimes I worry people might be able to place thoughts in my head, or take my thoughts away. But with Mum, there's nothing.

'You're better than Dad.'

'Really?'

'He can't get past Level One.'

My mum is made of angles, and sharp corners of bone. She isn't great to cuddle. But she put a cushion on her lap for me to rest my head, and that was comfortable.

At lunchtime she made vegetable stew.

Usually we ate at the table, but this time we took our bowls into the den. I was starting to feel floppy and useless.

'Try and eat up, sweetheart.'

'It hurts to swallow.'

She looked in my throat and said my tonsils were still swollen, that she'd make a Lemsip after we'd eaten. She picked up my spoon, and fed me a mouthful, scooping a bit of spillage off my chin like you would for a baby. Then she said, 'Why more than one life?'

'What?'

'In computer games. It doesn't make sense, having lots of lives. It makes no sense at all.'

'It's just the way they are.'

She shook her head. 'I'm being silly, aren't I? Shall we play Snakes and Ladders next?'

I opened my mouth, and she fed me another spoonful. It wasn't a plastic spoon or anything. It wasn't for babies. It was a regular spoon.

mon ami

He used to burst through the door, waiting at the foot of my bed all wide-eyed and unblinking. Some mornings I wasn't in the mood so sent him away. I regret that now.

But mostly his enthusiasm was catching, so even if I was half asleep I'd get out of bed to load up the N64, and we'd sit on our beanbags playing Mario 64, arguing over whether Luigi could be unlocked as a character. Then at quarter to seven our dad would come through to tell us we should work hard at school today, and that he was off to earn a crust. That is the kind of thing my dad says. He says, earn a crust. I like it.

The other reason Dad used to come into my bedroom was so Simon and me could do this thing we used to do. What we'd do is listen out for him as he walked across the landing towards my bedroom door. He was easy to hear because he wore heavy steel-toe-capped boots, and because he wanted us to hear him. So he would walk deliberately heavy-footed, and usually say something loud and obvious to my mum like, 'Bye bye then darling. I'm just going to say cheerio to the boys.'

As soon as we heard him say that, Simon and me would quickly hide behind the door, so when he looked in he wouldn't be able to see us. He'd step inside pretending to be confused, saying something under his breath like, 'Where have those boys got to?'

It was stupid really, because by this time Simon wouldn't be able to stop from giggling. That didn't matter though, because we all knew it was just pretend. And it was fun. The most fun thing was at this point Simon and me would leap out from behind the door, and wrestle Dad to the ground.

That is what we used to do when Simon was alive, but now Simon wasn't alive, I never got up before my dad. At quarter to seven he would still come into my room to find me lying awake, unsure of how to begin. That must have been hard for him.

He came in every morning anyway, to sit beside me for a few minutes and just be there.

'Morning mon ami, you okay?' He ruffled my hair, in that way grown-ups do to children, and we did our special handshake. 'You going to work hard for Mummy today?'

I nodded, yes.

'Good lad. Work hard then you can get a decent job and look after your old pa, eh?'

'I will mon ami.'

———

It started in France when I was five years old. This was our only holiday abroad, and Mum had won it in a magazine competition. It was something to be proud of, first prize in a True Lives writing contest, eight hundred words or less about what makes your family special. She wrote about the struggles and rewards of raising a child with Down Syndrome. I don't suppose I got a mention. The judges loved it.

Some people can remember way back to the beginning of their lives. I've even met people who say they can remember being born.

The farthest back my mind can reach puts me standing in a rock pool, with my dad holding one of my hands for balance, in the other I'm clutching my brand new net, and we are catching fish together. It isn't a whole memory. I just keep a few fragments; a cold slice of water just below my knees, seagulls, a boat in the distance – that sort of thing. Dad can remember more. He can remember that we talked, and what we talked about. A five-year-old boy and his daddy chewing the cud over everything from the size of the sea to where the sun goes at night. And whatever I said in that rock pool, it was enough for my dad to like me. So that was that. We became friends. But because we were in France we became amis. I don't suppose any of this matters. I just wanted to remind myself.

———

'Right then. I'm off to earn that crust.'

'Do you have to go, Dad?'

'Only until we win the lottery, eh?' Then he winked at me (but not in a Steve way) and we did our special handshake again. 'Work hard for Mummy.'

Mum wore her long nightdress and the silly animal slippers Simon had once chosen for her birthday. 'Morning baby boy.'

'Tell me about France again, Mum.'

She stepped into my room and opened the curtains, so that for a moment, standing in front of the window, she became nothing but a faceless silhouette. Then she said it again. Just like before. 'Sweetheart, you look pale.'

school runs

I think of Mum zipping closed my orange winter coat again, and pulling up the hood again so the grey fur lining clings to the sweat on my forehead and brushes at my ears. I think of it, and it is happening. Hot honey and lemon drunk down in gulps from the mug I once gave to her – no longer special – and a bitter chalky after-taste of ground-up paracetamol.

'I'm sorry about the other day, sweetheart.'

'Sorry for what, Mummy?'

'For dragging you past the playground, with the other children staring.'

'Were you punishing me?'

'I don't know. I might have been. I'm not sure.'

'Do we have to do it again?'

'I think so, yes. You have your coat on.'

'You put it on me. You zipped it up.'

'Did I?'

'Yes.'

'Then we should go.'

'I don't want to.'

'I know that, Matthew. But you're unwell, and you might need antibiotics. We need to get you seen. Did I really zip your coat up?'

'But why now? Why can't we wait until after playtime has finished?'

'I don't know. I haven't worked that out yet.'

I pass her back the empty mug, World's Greatest Mum. I think of this and I am there again. She's opening the door, reaching out her hand. I take it, and I am there.

'No!'

'Matthew, don't answer me back. We need to go. We need to get you seen.'

'No. I want Dad.'

'Don't be silly, he's at work. Now you're letting all the cold air inside. Stop it. We need to go.'

Her grip is tight, but I'm stronger than she thinks. I pull back hard, and snag at her charm bracelet with the hook of my finger.

'Now look what you've done. It's broken.' She bends over to pick up the fallen chain, with its tiny silver charms littering the ground. I push past her. I push her harder than I should. She loses balance, arms flapping like pigeon wings before she falls. 'Matthew! Wait! What is it?'

In a few strides I'm through the gate, slamming it behind me. I run as fast as I can, but she's catching up. My foot skids off the pavement, I'm startled by the urgent blast from a speeding van.

'Baby, wait. Please.'

'No.'

I take my chance, running across the main road, cutting between a line of cars, causing one to swerve. She's forced to wait. I round the corner, and the next, and am at my school. 'Is that you again, Matthew? Hey, it's Matthew again. Look, his mum's chasing him. His mum's chasing him. Look! His mum's chasing him!'

I am ahead, and she is chasing. She's crying out for me to stop. She's calling me her baby. She's calling me her baby boy. I stop. Turn around. Then fall into her arms.

'Look at them. Look at them. Get a teacher, someone. Look at them.' I am lifted from the ground, held by her. She is kissing my forehead and telling me that it will be okay. She's carrying me, and I can feel her heartbeat through my stupid hood.

'I'm so sorry, Mum. I'm so sorry.'

'It's okay baby boy.'

'I miss him so much, Mum.'

'I know you do. Oh, my baby. I know you do.' She's carrying me, and I can feel her heartbeat through my stupid hood.

Children must be accompanied by an adult
AT ALL TIMES

In Bristol there is a famous bridge called the Clifton Suspension Bridge. It's a popular hangout for the suicidal. There is even a notice on it with a telephone number for the Samaritans.

When my mum first left school, before she met Dad, she worked doing paper filing at Rolls-Royce.

It wasn't a happy time because her boss was a horrible man who made her feel stupid and worthless. She wanted to quit, but was too worried to tell Granddad because he had wanted her to stay at school, and having a job was a condition of her leaving.

She was riding back on her moped one evening, but when she reached home she didn't stop.

'I kept going,' she told me. She perched on the edge of my bed in her nightgown, having woken me in the middle of the night to climb in beside me. She did that a lot.

'I had nothing to live for,' she whispered.

'Are you okay, Mummy?'

She didn't know that she was going to the suspension bridge, but she was. She only realized, when she couldn't find it.

'I was lost.'

'Should I get Dad?'

'Let's go to sleep.'

'Are you sleeping here tonight?'

'Am I allowed?'

'Of course.'

'I was lost,' she whispered into the pillow. 'I couldn't even get that right.'

dead people still have birthdays

The night before my dead brother should have turned thirteen years old I was woken by the sound of him playing in his bedroom.

I was getting better at picturing him in my mind. So I kept my eyes closed and watched as he reached beneath his bed and pulled out the painted cardboard box.

These were his keepsakes, but if you're like Simon, and the whole world is a place of wonder, everything is a keepsake. There were countless small plastic toys from Christmas crackers and McDonald's Happy Meals. There were stickers from the dentist saying, *I was brave*, and stickers from the speech therapist saying, *Well Done*, or *You are a Star!* There were postcards from Granddad and Nanny Noo – if his name was on it, it was going in his box. There were swimming badges, certificates, a fossil from Chesil Beach, good pebbles, paintings, pictures, birthday cards, a broken watch – so much crap he could hardly close the lid.

Simon kept every single day of his life.

*

It was strange to think of it all still there. In some ways it was strange even to think of his room being there. I remember when we first got home from Ocean Cove, the three of us stood in the driveway, listening to the little clicking sounds as the car's engine cooled. We stared at the house. His room had stayed put, the first-floor window, with his yellow Pokémon curtains. It hadn't the courtesy to up and leave. It stayed right where we'd left it, at the top of the stairs, the room next to mine.

Hugging a pillow to my chest and keeping my eyes shut tight, I could see him searching through his memories to find the most important one – a scrap of yellow cotton. It was this he was first wrapped in as a tiny bundle of joy and fear, and it became his comfort blanket. At seven, eight, nine years of age – he always had it with him, forever carrying it around. Until the day I told him that he looked like a baby. I told him he looked like a little baby with his little baby blanket, that if he wasn't so thick all the time he'd understand. It disappeared after that, everyone proudly accepting he'd outgrown it.

I lay listening to him, sleep drifting back over me as he climbed into his bed. Then breaking through, not enough to wake me, but at the very edge of my awareness, another sound – Mum was singing him a lullaby.

Spring sunshine painted pillars of white across my carpet.

It was Saturday, which meant breakfast around the table. I put on my dressing gown, but didn't go downstairs straight away. I wanted to check something first.

This wasn't the first time I'd been in his room.

Dad hadn't wanted me to feel afraid or weird about anything, so after I got back from staying with Nanny Noo, we went in together. We shuffled around awkwardly and Dad said something about how he knew Simon wouldn't mind if I played with his toys.

People always think they know what dead people would and wouldn't mind, and it's always the same as what *they* would and wouldn't mind – like this time at school when a really naughty boy, Ashley Stone, died of Meningitis. We had this special assembly for him which even his mum attended, where Mr Rogers talked about how *spirited* and *playful* Ashley was, and how we'd always remember him with love. Then he said he was certain Ashley would want us to try and be brave, and to work hard. But I don't think Ashley would have wanted that at all, and maybe that's because I didn't want it. So you see what I mean? But I suppose Dad was right. Simon wouldn't mind if I played with his toys because he never minded. I didn't play with them though, and the reason is the obvious one. I felt too guilty. Some things in life are exactly as we imagine.

His model aeroplanes swung gently on their strings, and the radiator creaked and groaned. I stood beside his bed lifting the comfort blanket from his pillow. 'Hey Si,' I whispered. 'Happy birthday.' Then I placed the blanket back in his keepsake box, and closed the lid.

I guess children believe whatever they want to believe.

Perhaps adults do too.

In the kitchen Dad was making a start on breakfast, prodding bacon around a sizzling pan. 'Morning, mon ami.'

'Where's Mum?'

'Bacon sandwich?'

'Where's Mum?'

'She didn't sleep well, sunshine. Bacon sandwich?'

'I want marmalade, I think.' I opened the cupboard, pulled out a jar and struggled with the lid before handing it to Dad.

'You must have loosened it for me, eh?'

He lifted a rasher, considered it, and dropped it back in the pan. 'Are you sure you don't want bacon? I'm having bacon.'

'We go to the doctor's a lot, Dad.'

'Ouch. Shit!'

He glared at the reddened flesh on his knuckle, as though expecting it to say sorry.

'Did you burn yourself, Daddy?'

'It's not so bad.' Stepping to the sink, he turned on the cold tap and made a comment about how untidy the garden looked. I scooped out four large spoonfuls of marmalade, emptying it. 'Can I keep this?'

'The jar? What for?'

'Will you keep your voices down?' The door swung open hard, banging against the table. 'I need some bloody sleep. Please let me sleep today.'

She didn't say it in an angry way, more like pleading. She closed the door again, slowly this time, and as I listened to her footsteps climbing the stairs, I felt a horrible emptiness in my tummy –

the kind that breakfast can't fill.

'It's okay sunshine,' Dad said, forcing a smile, 'You didn't do anything. Today's a bit difficult. How about you finish up your breakfast and I'll go talk to her, eh?'

He said that like it was a question, but it wasn't. What he meant was that I had no choice but to stay put, whilst he followed her upstairs. But I didn't want to sit by myself at the table again, or listen to another muffled argument throbbing through the walls. Besides, I had something to do. I picked up the marmalade jar and stepped out of the back door into our garden.

These are the memories that crawl under my skin. Simon had wanted an Ant Farm, and dead people still have birthdays.

Crouching beside the tool shed with mud between my toes, I lifted large flat stones like Granddad had taught me. But it was too early in the year, so even under the bigger slabs I could only find earthworms and beetles. I looked deeper, digging a hole with my fingers – as the first drops of rain hit my dressing gown, I was somewhere else: *It's dark, night-time, the air tastes of salt, and Simon is beside me, wiping rain from his cheeks and bleating that he doesn't like it any more, that he doesn't like it and wants to go back. I keep digging, telling him to stop being a baby, to hold the torch still, and he holds it with trembling hands, until her button eyes glisten in the beam.*

'Matthew, sweetheart!' Mum was standing at her bedroom window calling out, 'It's pouring down!'

As I opened the back door, the front door slammed shut.

I ran upstairs.

'Sweetheart, what are we going to do with you?' She took my wet dressing gown, wrapping me in a towel.

'Where did Dad go?'

'He's gone for a walk.'

'It's raining.'

'I doubt he'll be long.'

'I wanted us all to have breakfast together.'

'I'm so tired, Matthew.'

We sat beside each other on the bed, watching the rain against the window.

a different story

Only fifteen minutes today, then puncture time. I have a few compliance problems with tablets, the answer – a long, sharp needle.

Every other week, alternate sides.

I'd rather not think about it now. It's best not to think until the injection is actually going in.

I want to tell a story. When *Click-Click-Wink* Steve first got me started on the computer, he said I could use the printer as well. 'To share your writing with us, Matt. Or take it home to keep safe.'

Except the other day the printer didn't work. I'd been thinking about the time Mum took me to see Dr Marlow, but we saw a different GP instead. I couldn't remember the details, like what exactly my mum thought was wrong with me, or why Dr Marlow wasn't there. So I made something up about the mole beside my nipple, and Dr Marlow being on holiday. Perhaps that was even true, it's not important. The important part was this new doctor

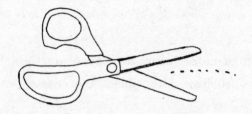

asked to speak with Mum in private, and their conversation was the beginning of **a whole new chapter** in our lives. But when I tried to print this, an error message flashed up and no paper came out.

So that was that.

Until this morning at Art Group – where whispery Jeanette gives out bottles of poster paint, glue, knackered old felt tips and tissue paper, and we are supposed to express ourselves. I sat beside Patricia, who must be sixty years old, or maybe even older, but wears a long blonde wig and pretends to be twenty. She wears dark sunglasses, bright pink lipstick, and today she's wearing her bright pink catsuit too. She usually draws colourful patterns in crayon, which Jeanette says are beautiful. But this morning she was doing something else, quietly absorbed, making precise cuts into sheets of paper with a pair of blunt scissors, then carefully arranging the cut-out pieces onto a square of cardboard.

I suppose the printer must have finally coughed up my pages, and they ended up with the scrap paper. It was a strange feeling, and for a moment I wanted to shout, but I didn't because Patricia's a really nice person and I think if she'd known it was my writing, she wouldn't have taken it. She shook her head, turning away from me slightly; **PLEASE STOP READING OVER MY SHOULDER**. You can see why this was different, though? But I didn't want to upset her, so I carried on doing my sketches, whilst she carried on rearranging my life, sticking it down with Pritt Stick.

I waited until just before the end of the hour, when we have a few minutes to share what we've done with the group, but I knew

Patricia wouldn't, because even though she wears those clothes, she's actually very shy.

'I'll clean the brushes,' I offered.

'Is it that time already?' asked Jeanette.

I want to tell a different story, a story belonging to someone else. It will not be the same as mine, and though it might be sad in some ways, it will also be happy because in the end there are beautiful crayon patterns and a lady with long blonde hair who stays twenty years old forever.

I moved around the table collecting paintbrushes, and glanced over her shoulder. What we can know about Patricia's story, is that she's

trapped.

in   two framed photographs

self-conscious

eyes darting between

– the younger one

this

and

old

body,

the end

second opinion

She ran the tip of her finger over the small dark mole beside my
nipple, and I felt my face grow hot.

'It doesn't itch?'

'No.'

'Has it grown or changed colour?'

'I don't think so.'

'We usually see Dr Marlow,' Mum offered for the third time.

I pulled my top on and shrank into the chair, self-conscious of
my changing body, of how it had started to stretch and stink and
grow wisps of hair, so that with each passing day I knew myself
a little less.

'How old are you, Matthew?'

'He's ten,' my mum answered.

'I'm nearly eleven,' I said.

She turned back to the computer screen, scanning appointment after appointment. I stared absently at the two framed
photographs of Dr Marlow's daughters – the younger one riding
her horse, and her sister in graduation robes, grinning, with eyes

half closed – and I wondered if this new doctor would get her own office, and have pictures of her own family for me to stare at every couple of weeks, until I felt I'd met them.

'How are you getting on at school?'

'What?'

She was looking right at me, not buried in a prescription sheet or tapping on her keyboard, but looking right at me, leaning forwards.

Mum coughed, and said she thought my mole had grown, but maybe it hadn't.

'You must be starting secondary school after the holidays?'

I wanted to turn to Mum for reassurance, but there was something about how the doctor was leaning forwards that held me. I don't mean I felt trapped. I mean I felt held.

'I don't go to school.'

'No?'

'We home tutor,' Mum said. Then, 'I used to be a teacher.'

The doctor kept looking at me. She had placed her chair near to mine, and now I found myself leaning forward as well. It's difficult to explain, but in that moment I felt safe, as though I could say anything I wanted.

I didn't say anything though.

The doctor nodded.

'I don't think there's anything to worry about with the mole, Matthew. Do you?'

I shook my head.

Mum was on her feet, already saying thank you, already

ushering me to the door, then the doctor said, 'I wonder if perhaps we might be able to talk in private for a moment?'

I felt Mum's grip tighten on my arm, her eyes darting between
us. 'But. I'm his mother.'

'Sorry, no. I wasn't clear Susan. I wonder if you and I might
talk in private for a moment?' She then turned to me and said, 'It's
really nothing to worry about, Matthew.'

The receptionist was telling a woman with a pushchair how Dr
Marlow was on holiday until the end of the month, but a young
lady doctor was covering and she was very nice, and they even
hoped she might stay on. I sat on the rubber mat in the corner,
where they keep toys for children. I guess I was too old really,
and after a while of glaring at me and sighing heavily, the woman
asked whether I'd mind making room for her *child* to play.

'Can I play with him?'

'Oh.'

Her little boy reached out a hand, and I gave him a Stickle
Brick, which he dropped to the floor and laughed like it was the
funniest thing to ever happen. I picked it up and we did it again,
this time his mum laughed too and said, 'He's bonkers, I tell you,
absolutely bonkers.'

'I've got a brother.'

'Oh, right?'

'Yeah. He was older than me. We were good mates. But he's
dead and stuff now.'

'Oh. I see. I'm sorry—'

The bell chimed and a name scrolled across the sign by

reception. 'That's us I'm afraid. Come on mister.' She picked up her little boy and he immediately began to whimper, stretching his arms back towards me.

'Someone's made a new friend,' she said, before rushing him down the corridor.

'I've got a brother,' I said again to no one in particular. 'But I don't think about him so much any more.'

I put the Stickle Bricks away.

Mum appeared, pressing a prescription sheet into her handbag.

'Is everything okay, Mum?'

'Let's get ice creams.'

I don't suppose it was the best weather for the park – it was pretty cold and cloudy. But we went anyway. Mum bought us ice creams from the van, and we perched on the swings next to each other. 'I've not been a very good Mummy, have I?'

'Is that what the doctor said?'

'I worry, Matthew. I worry all the time.'

'Do you need medicine?'

'I might.'

'Are you and Dad going to get divorced?'

'Sweetheart, why would you even think that?'

'I don't know. Are you?'

'Of course not.' She finished her ice cream, stepped off the swing, and started to push mine.

'I'm not a baby, Mum.'

'I know, sorry. I know. Sometimes I think you're more grown up than me.'

'No you don't.'

'I do. And you're definitely too clever for me now. You do those exercise books quicker than I can mark them.'

'I don't.'

'You do, sweetheart. I think if you went back to school, the teachers wouldn't know what hit them.'

'Really?'

'Really.'

'I'm allowed?'

'Is it what you want?'

This might not have happened so quickly as I'm telling it, or reached the surface of our conversation so easily. Probably we were in the park for a very long time, drifting in and out of silences, each moving around an idea, afraid to reach out and see it sink away, and this time, to impossible depths. No. It didn't happen quickly or easily. But it did happen. On that day. In that park.

'It isn't that I don't like you teaching me—'

'I know. It's okay. I know.'

'We could still do lessons in the evenings.'

'I'll help with your homework.'

'And you'll still help me type up my stories?'

'If you'll let me. I'd like that a lot.'

A good thing about talking to someone who is standing behind you is that you can pretend you don't know they're crying, and not trouble yourself too much with working out why. You can simply concentrate on helping them feel better.

'You can push me if you want, Mum.'

'Oh I can push you now, can I?'

'If you want.'

She did, she pushed me on the swing, higher and higher, and when at last the grey clouds parted for the sun to shine through, it was like it was shining just for us.

a whole new chapter

'Uh, what? Hey mon ami.'

'Can you help me do my tie up, Dad?'

'What time is it?'

Mum turned over in bed, and pulled off her eye mask. 'Matthew, it's the middle of the night.'

'I don't know how to do it up. Can I turn the light on?'

I pressed the switch and they both groaned, then Dad said, through a yawn, 'Usually you put a shirt on first, mate.'

'I just want to practise.'

'We can practise in the morning, before I go to work.' He rolled over, pulling the quilt above his head. 'It's the middle of the night.'

I switched their light off and went back to my room, grappling with the knot – too nervous to sleep. It wasn't so long before Mum came through to sit with me though. I knew she would. I knew she would come and sit with me if I woke them.

'You need to get some sleep, darling.'

'What if no one likes me?'

I didn't know who was most worried about me going back to

school – me or her. She had her little yellow pills though, which took the edge off.

'Of course they will.' She stroked the hair behind my ear, like she used to when I was little, 'Of course they will.'

'But what if they don't?'

She told me the story about her first day at secondary school, of how she had broken her arm in the summer holiday so was wearing a plaster cast. She said there were so many new faces, but the new faces were feeling exactly the same as she was. By lunch-time her plaster cast was scrawled with well-wishing messages from her brand new group of friends.

'What happened next?'

'It's cold, let me in.'

I pulled back my covers and budged over so she could climb in beside me.

'This is the good part,' she said, propping up a pillow. 'One of the playground monitors saw my plaster cast with the writing, and wanted me punished for breaking school uniform rules! So my very first day I was marched to the headmistress, who thanked the monitor for her concerns, looked at my cast, picked up a pen, and wrote Welcome to Pen Park High.'

It was a good story, I suppose.

If it was true.

FUCK IT

I haven't been feeling too good these last couple of days.

This is far more difficult than I thought. Thinking about the past is like digging up graves.

Once-upon-a-time we buried the memories we didn't want. We found a little patch of grass at Ocean Cove Holiday Park, beside the recycling bins, or further up the path near to the shower blocks, and we kept hold of the memories we wanted, and we buried the rest.

But coming to this place every Monday, Wednesday, and Friday, spending half my life with NUTTERS like Patricia, and the Asian guy in the relaxation room, slyly pocketing pieces from the jigsaw puzzles and rocking backwards and forwards like he's a pendulum, and the skinny BITCH who skips along the corridor singing God Will Save Us, God Will Save Us, when all I want to do is concentrate, but can't because the stuff they inject makes me twitch and contort, and fills my mouth with so much saliva I'm actually drooling onto the fucking keyboard – I'm just saying this is harder than I thought.

'The thing is Mum, it wasn't the same for you, was it?'

'In some ways—'

'No. It wasn't. It wasn't the same because Nanny Noo didn't stop you going to school in the first place, or make you sit by your-self for a whole year making pretend mistakes in your exercise books and wondering when—'

'Matthew, no. I didn't—'

'Wondering when I would have to go to the doctor's, if you'd drag me there past the whole school, staring and pointing—'

'Matthew, please—'

'Staring and pointing at me—'

'It wasn't like—'

'It was! It was just like that. And you made it like that. So now I have to see them all again. I don't care about the new people. I don't care about the people who don't know me. I don't care about not having anyone to write on a stupid plaster cast. I don't—'

'Matthew, please listen to me.'

She tried to put her arms around me but I pulled away. 'No. I don't have to listen. I don't have to listen any more. I'm never going to listen to you. I don't care what you think.'

'You need to get some sleep, Matt.'

She wobbled a bit as she got to her feet, and for a second looked down at me as though balanced on a cliff edge.

I had one more thing to say, but I didn't want to shout it. I forced each word into a tightly bound whisper.

'I hate you.'

Mum closed my door softly behind her.

handshakes

I didn't describe the special handshake I do with Dad.

When we became *amis* we decided on a handshake. I think I've mentioned it already, but I didn't say how it goes. It's a special handshake, not a secret handshake. So I can tell you.

What we do is reach out with our left hands and link our fingers, then we touch the tips of our thumbs together. We must have done this thousands of times.

I haven't counted.

Each special handshake takes a brief second, but if each one was placed end to end they would stretch for hours.

If somebody took a photograph every time, at the precise moment our thumbs touch, and viewed the photographs in a flip book, it would make a time-lapse film – like you get on wildlife programmes to see plants grow, or weeds creeping across a forest floor.

The film begins with a five-year-old boy, on holiday with his family in France. He's been trying to delay bedtime by talking to his dad about the hermit crab they caught in the rock pool.

The handshake was his dad's idea. Their thumbs touch, and the camera clicks. In the background, on the hotel balcony, the boy's Mum and older brother look on. They reveal a hint of pride, and jealousy.

Day and night flash in a strobe, seasons collide, clouds explode, candles melt onto icing sugar, a wreath rots way. The boy and his dad rush through time, thumbs pressed together.

The boy grows like a weed.

And in every moment is a world unseen – beyond balconies, outside of memory, far from the reach of understanding.

I can only describe reality as I know it. I'm doing my best, and promise to keep trying. Shake on it.

prodrome *n.* an early symptom that
a disease is developing.

There is weather and there is climate.

If it rains outside, or if you stab a classmate's shoulder with a compass needle, over and over, until his white cotton school shirt looks like blotting paper, that is the weather.

But if you live in a place where it is often likely to rain, or your perception falters and dislocates so that you retreat, suspicious and afraid of those closest to you, that is the climate.

These are the things we learnt at school.

I have an illness, a disease with the shape and sound of a snake. Whenever I learn something new, it learns it too.

If you have HIV or Cancer, or Athlete's Foot, you can't teach them anything. When Ashley Stone was dying of Meningitis, he might have known that he was dying, but his Meningitis didn't know. Meningitis doesn't know anything. But my illness knows everything that I know. This was a difficult thing to get my head around, but the moment I understood it, my illness understood it too.

These are the things we learnt.

We learnt about atoms.

This illness and me.

I was thirteen.

'STOP THAT, STOP THAT AT ONCE!'

His face turned purple, and a thick vein started throbbing on the side of his neck. Mr Philips was the sort of teacher who wanted lessons to be fun. It took a lot to make him angry.

Jacob Greening could manage though. I can't remember what he was doing, exactly. This was in science, so probably it had something to do with the gas taps. In the science block there were these gas taps on the tables for fuelling Bunsen burners. It might have been that Jacob put his mouth over one of them and was sucking at the gas to see what would happen – it might have been his face that was turning purple, his neck veins throbbing. Perhaps he was set to exhale it onto a lighter flame, to breathe fire.

Jacob wanted to make lessons fun too.

We'd met on the very first day.

It happened like this:

Dad had taught me to knot my tie, as promised. Jacob turned up to school without one. In registration he started whispering into my ear, as though we'd known each other for years. He was going on about needing to see the Head Teacher, how it was private, and really important. I didn't listen properly. My mind kept taking me back to what I'd said to Mum, about hating her. She'd driven me to school in silence. I pressed my face against the cool glass, and she flicked through radio stations. I'd hurt her

feelings, and was trying to decide if I cared. Jacob was still talking, only now I realized he was anxious. His words were tripping
over each other. He had to see the Head Teacher, but he didn't
have a tie. That was the crux of it.

'You can have mine if you want.'

'Can I?'

I gave him my tie and he wrapped it inside his collar, then
looked at me helplessly. So I knotted it for him. I turned down his
collar and tucked the end inside his shirt. I suppose it made us
friends. He sat next to me in lessons but at breaks he'd be gone,
bolting through the school gates with his rucksack held tight to
one shoulder, and his anorak flapping in the wind. He had special
permission to go home. This wasn't something he talked about.

Mr Philips crashed a fist onto our table, 'It's not good enough
Jacob! This constant childish, dangerous behaviour—'

'Sorry sir.' Even as he said it, a smile crept across his acned
face. It is strange how fast we change – he wasn't the sort to give
a shit about school ties any more.

'Get out! Get out of my classroom!'

He slowly moved to pack his stuff away.

'Leave your bag. You can get it after the bell.'

'But—'

'Out! Now!'

The problem with sitting next to Jacob was that whenever he
drew attention to himself, everyone looked at me too. I felt a surge
of anger towards him then. Here is a question:

What do you have in common with Albert Einstein?
1) You are made out of similar kinds of atoms
2) You are made out of the same kind of atoms
3) You are partly made out of **THE SAME** atoms

Jacob Greening slammed shut the door behind him, and Mr Philips asked that we all settle down again and look at the whiteboard. It is a good question, I think.

'I'd like you all to decide which statement you think is true, and write down one, two or three in the back of your exercise books.'

'Sir?'

'Yes Sally.'

'What if we don't know, sir?'

'I don't expect you to know. We're going to work it out together. Let me ask you another question. How much do you think I weigh?'

'What?' Sally shrugged, and I imagined how it might be to kiss her neck, or what her tits would feel like.

'Have a guess.'

'About twelve stone?'

'Good guess.'

Sally smiled, then saw me staring. You're weird, she mouthed silently. I turned away and picked up Jacob's pencil case. He was the kind of boy who drew knobs on his own pencil case.

I never worked him out.

Mr Philips stood beside the whiteboard. 'I weigh nearer to

eleven and a half stone, or seventy-four kilograms, which means I have approximately, 7.4×10^{27} atoms in my body.'

That is a way of abbreviating really huge numbers. Here is the number written out in full:

7,400,000,000,000,000,000,000,000,000

Jacob was kicking the wall in the corridor. Sally was copying out the zeros. Someone else was looking out of the window. Someone else was imagining their future. Someone else could feel the start of a headache. Someone else needed a piss. Someone else was trying to keep up. Someone else was bored and angry. Someone else was somewhere else, and Mr Philips was saying, 'This is more than every single grain of sand on every single beach.'

It

is

more

than

all

the

STARS

in

the

entire

UNIVERSE

These are the things we learnt.

My illness and I.

'Billions of years ago exploding stars sent atoms hurtling through space and we've been recycling them on Earth ever since. Except for the occasional comet, meteor, some interstellar dust, we've used exactly the same atoms over and over since the Earth was formed. We eat them, we drink them, we breathe them, we are made of them. At this precise moment each of us is exchanging our atoms with everyone else, and not just with each other, but with other animals, trees, fungi, moulds—'

Mr Philips glanced at the clock, it was nearly break time, and already people had started to pack away their books and begin conversations.

'Quiet please. We're nearly done. So what do you have in common with Einstein? One. Are you made out of similar kinds of atoms? Yes, I suppose, and aside from the most minute variations all humans are made of the same basic ingredients, Oxygen (sixty-five per cent), Carbon (eighteen per cent), Hydrogen (ten per cent) etc. So number two is also correct, but what about number three? Is there any part of the world's greatest ever physicist sitting amongst us now?'

He looked around the room, pausing for effect. 'Sadly, not enough it seems. For those who are interested, the answer is yes, and not just one or two atoms, but probably many many many atoms that were once part of Einstein, are currently, for a while at least, part of you. Right now. And not just Einstein, but Julius Caesar, Hitler, the cavemen, dinosaurs—'

The bell rang, cutting his list short.

I added someone else though.

Jacob rushed into the classroom, grabbed his bag, and left, ignoring Mr Philips' request for him to stay. I don't know why it was this day I decided to follow him. Perhaps it wasn't. Perhaps it was another day.

Maybe I waited in the rain, hidden beside the bike sheds – which aren't really sheds, but more like a cage – and after he ran through the gates, gasping at air, I ran after him. It wasn't so far; a few streets onto the estate with the small bungalows and little squares of perfectly kept green lawn.

It was just a thing to do, I suppose – to see where he lived. Probably I'd turn around and head back as soon as he went inside.

'Jacob!'

Except I didn't head back.

I called out.

More and more these days I only knew what I was going to do as I actually did it. He was inside the porch. 'Jacob!' My voice was lost in the wind. He closed the door, and I stood on the front grass for a while, catching my breath.

The rain fell harder. I pulled up my hood and moved around the side of the bungalow. It was small, like a Doll's House. I don't mean it wasn't nice, that isn't what I'm saying. Anyway, not everything has to mean something.

I carefully stepped over a few empty plant pots and a garden gnome holding a fishing rod. This wasn't sneaking. You couldn't say I was sneaking, because I had tried to get his attention.

I had called out his name.

I think.

Around the back I arrived at the single large window, with its slatted blinds. I crouched down low, gripping the wet ledge with my fingers.

The electric wheelchair was the first thing I saw, but she wasn't in it. She was in bed, and now Jacob was beside her, leaning over her, attaching clips to a kind of metal crane. He stood back, holding a remote control. Slowly, she started to lift away from her mattress, hoisted in a huge sling. Jacob's movements were precise, efficient. Holding the top of the crane with both hands he swivelled her away from the bed, pulled away dirty sheets, put fresh ones in their place. I stopped watching him, because I couldn't take my eyes off her. The way he'd turned her, she was suspended facing the window, facing me, with her bloated arms flopped to her sides, her dull eyes fixed straight ahead.

It's dark, night-time, the air tastes of salt, and Simon is bleating, begging me not to dig it up, telling me he's frightened. I lift the doll, she is dirty, sodden. Her arms flop at her sides. I hold her in the air. The rain falls, and Simon is backing away, clutching his chest. She wants to play with you, Simon. She wants to play chase.

I ran, skidding around the side of the bungalow, tumbling over a stone pot, back on my feet, over the lawn – afraid to look back – across the road, through the gates, into school, with trillions of atoms colliding inside me, only atoms, trillions of atoms, and many, many, many of Simon's atoms. Somewhere in the playground I crumpled. And threw up.

*

Perhaps we had Geography that same day. Or maybe we didn't. Maybe it was another day.

The teacher put on a video, about the weather and the climate. Do you remember the difference? The lights were off to help us see the screen better, so I don't think Jacob noticed me reach into his pencil case and take out the set of compasses. I've already said what happened next. Sorry, Jacob.

the watching stair

'My God, listen to yourself. You sound like your father. So that's the answer, is it? You're going to what, Richard? Knock some sense into him?'

'You think I won't?'

'What will that teach him exactly?'

'That he can't bloody—'

'Go on.'

'Christ, Susan. We can't do nothing.'

'I'm not suggesting that.'

They were sitting in the glow of the standing lamp, holding hands, still holding hands even as they fought over what to do about a son like me. Mum's head resting on Dad's shoulder, a second bottle of wine nearly drunk.

'Then what exactly?'

'He knows what he did was wrong—'

'That doesn't cut it.'

'We're going to the school—'

'Yes, because we've been summoned.'

'No, because we offered. He's a teenage boy. They go through phases. Didn't you?'

'Not that phase. Not the phase of assaulting people.'

'It wasn't—'

'Now you listen to yourself. This isn't normal, it isn't part of growing up. And do you know what hurts the most?'

'You're disappointed, I know. So am I—'

'No, that isn't it. I was disappointed when he swore at your mother. I was disappointed when his school marks dropped and he didn't seem to care. I was disappointed when we caught him smoking, and again when we caught him smoking pot. I'd be hard pushed to recall a day this last year when I haven't been disappointed in the boy for something. But this?'

'Let's not do this now.'

'I'm ashamed.'

———

Simon used to stay up half an hour later than me, because he was the eldest. I'd brush my teeth and be tucked into bed, but when I was certain Mum had gone downstairs, I would follow.

On the fourth stair from the top, with your forehead pressed against the banisters, you can spy through a glass panel over the living-room door and see most of the sofa, half the coffee table, and a corner of the fireplace. I would watch until the darkness of the hall closed around the glow from the living room, and the softness of their voices blended with the sound of my own breathing, so that sometimes I wouldn't even feel myself being lifted, or hear Mum calling me her little rascal. I'd simply wake up the next morning, in the warm comfort of my own bed.

One night Simon was practising his reading. It wasn't so long before that this had been a shared ritual, the two of us taking turns to read aloud from the same book.

'It's my page, Matthew. Not yours.'

'I'm only trying to help.'

'I can do it by myself.'

He couldn't. Not so well. So he practised with Mum after I went to bed, and I'd watch her patiently teach him the same words night after night; she couldn't have loved him more. Dad would be relegated to the far end of the sofa where I couldn't see him properly, only his legs stretched out in front, and a socked foot resting on the coffee table.

That's how it was as Simon read his picture book of The Lion King. Nanny Noo bought it for him from a charity shop and it became his favourite because when it gets to the part where Pumbaa and Timon start talking about Hakuna Matata, Dad would try to sing it. It was so funny because he didn't know the words properly, and he'd always get partway through, then find himself doing that King of the Swingers song – which isn't even from The Lion King. I guess you had to be there, but it was really funny.

Except this night, as I sat on the watching stair, they didn't get that far, because when Simba's dad died in the buffalo stampede, Simon went quiet.

'What's the matter, sweetheart?'

'What if Daddy dies?'

I couldn't see Dad properly. It was hard to hear him too. But you get to know the sort of answer someone might give. What my dad would have done was make his funny face with his eyes all wide, and say something like, 'Blimey, sunshine. D'you know something your old pa doesn't?'

Usually that would be enough to make everything okay, but this time it wasn't, because Simon said it again. 'What if you die? What if— What if you both die?'

If he got himself wound up he'd struggle to get his breath, and that made things worse. Before I was born there was a time when he couldn't breathe for so long that his skin turned blue. That's what Mum told me, anyway. And even as she explained how he'd had a small operation, so it should never happen again, even as she told me that, she looked afraid.

'Who would— What would—'

He was clutching at his chest. I must have looked like a super-hero, bursting through the door – my dressing gown billowing like a cape. It was probably the shock that startled him out of it, and I'm not sure he even heard what I said, but what I said was, 'I'll look after you Simon. I'll always look after you.'

We read the rest of the story as a family. And when it got to Hakuna Matata, we all sang King of the Swingers. I've never seen my parents look so proud.

———

Dad gulped back the last of his wine, and went to refill his glass. Mum placed her hand over his.

'We're tired. Let's go to bed.'

'I'm ashamed of my own son.'

'Please, don't.'

'Well I am. And not for the first time.'

'What's that supposed to mean?'

'You know exactly what it means, don't pretend that you weren't too.'

'Don't you dare. How— You're drunk.'

'Am I?'

'Yes. You are. He's our little boy for Christ's sake.'

Dad slunk to the end of the sofa, and all I could see was his socked foot resting on the coffee table.

a cloud of smoke

Jacob fastened the clips on his side, and watched me fasten the clips on mine. 'It goes in the third notch,' he said.

I knew that already.

He liked to be sure.

When she was secure I took the remote control and pressed the ↑ button, jerking the mechanical arm into life, lifting her slowly into the air. 'It's so kind of you to help,' Mrs Greening said.

This was a good day for her, some days she didn't talk. I think Jacob preferred it when she didn't talk.

He emptied her bag of piss into a plastic jug, whilst I put fresh sheets on the bed and fluffed her pillows.

'I think I'll go in the chair today,' she said.

Jacob positioned the electric wheelchair, and supported her neck and head as I pressed the ↓ button. In the kitchen the microwave went *ping*, and he said, 'I'll go.' Then he disappeared to collect her tea.

'Do you know where your tray is?'

'Over there, on the bedside table.' She pointed, but even that

NATHAN FILER

was difficult for her. She had better days and worse days. On the really bad days, she found it hard to do almost anything.

I attached the tea-tray into the slot on the front of her chair, and she asked, 'Are you as good to your mother?'

'What? My mum isn't—'

We went quiet then, and time stretched out, endlessly.

She had a nice long neck but a crooked nose. I couldn't decide if she was prettier than Mum.

I don't suppose it matters.

'I mean—'

'Here you go, Ma.' Jacob came back through, placing her food onto the tray. 'Careful, it's hot.'

He'd seen me. Of course he'd seen me. Peeking through the window, watching him, looking at his mum, then running away. What difference does it make? Aren't we all desperate to spill our secrets?

I was suspended for two weeks. Mum and Dad and me were on one side of the desk, and the Deputy Head was on the other, saying, 'We cannot accept behaviour of this kind in our school, indeed in our society.'

My parents nodded.

I assume.

I was staring at my hands, too ashamed to look at anyone. Mum said how truly sorry I was, that I'd arrived home as white as a ghost, and the Deputy Head said she didn't doubt it, how her impression, indeed the impression of her staff, was of a quiet, reflective student.

I clenched my fists, digging little crescents into my palms with my fingernails. I could feel her staring at me, trying to read my thoughts. Perhaps there was something going on at home they should know about? Anything that might be troubling me?

My parents shook their heads.

I assume.

It doesn't matter because when I arrived back at school, and took my seat for morning registration, his grinning face appeared next to me. Jacob Greening wasn't the sort to hold grudges.

'Fuck it. Didn't hurt, anyway.'

I think it took a lot of courage for him to invite me round, but that's what he did. He said, 'I've got Grand Theft Auto if you want to play it?' So we started hanging out together after school. I couldn't seem to concentrate on games though, even ones I used to enjoy. It was the same in lessons. One minute I'd be listening, interested, taking everything in, the next my head would be completely empty.

What I was better at concentrating on, was helping out with Mrs Greening. This didn't happen straight away. For the first few weeks I'd wait in the kitchen whilst Jacob did whatever needed doing, but after a while I started to help out with the odd little thing, like making her beakers of tea, or helping her tune the radio to a station she wanted, whilst Jacob got on with crushing up her tablets, or whatever.

After a few months though, I helped with everything, and I suppose it was this that got me thinking. You're going to laugh, but I thought maybe, when I left school, I could be a doctor.

I know that's stupid.

I can see that now.

This isn't about sympathy. I've made people feel sorry for me before, mostly psychiatric nurses – either the newly qualified ones who haven't learnt to get a grip, or the gooey-eyed maternal ones who take one look at me and see what could have happened to their own. A student nurse once told me how my patient notes had nearly made her cry. I told her to go fuck herself. That finished the job off.

If I look at my hands, right now. If I look at my fingers jabbing at the keyboard, the hard patches of dark brown skin, tobacco-stained knuckles, bitten nails – it's hard to think I'm the same person. It is hard to believe these are the same hands that helped to turn Mrs Greening in her bed, that gently rubbed cream onto her skin sores, that helped to wash her and brush her hair.

'We'll be in my room, Ma.'

'Okay darling,' she said, lifting a spoonful of hot mush into her mouth, spilling gravy. 'Don't make too much noise.'

His bedroom walls were plastered in old flyers from early '90s raves like Helter Skelter and Fantazia. It was stupid because we were still babies when they were happening, but he used to go on about them, saying how dance music was much better *back in the day*, and how now it was too commercial. I think he liked to talk about it so he could remind me it was his big brother who had given him all the flyers, before he left to join the army.

I guess that was it.

He wasn't trying to sound clever, he just wanted to be able to talk about his brother – so I would talk about mine. I only just thought that. I only thought it as I wrote it.

Opening the wardrobe I carefully lifted out the bucket of water, with the sawn-off Coke bottle floating on a layer of ash. This was the other thing me and Jacob Greening did together. He rummaged through a drawer, pulling out what was left of our Ten Bag of skunk, and started loading up a pile onto the tinfoil gauze.

I don't know if you have ever smoked a Bucket Bong before, but this was something else his brother had shown him. 'To get you really fucking stoned.'

'Tell me what you did,' he said, out of nowhere.

'What?'

'You know what I'm talking about.'

'What?'

He held his lighter over the leaves, and gradually lifted the bottle through the water, filling the chamber with thick white smoke.

'Tell me about what happened, why you left your junior school, everyone talks about it, everyone says—'

'Everyone says what?'

He looked straight at me, sort of startled. Then said, 'Fuck it, eh? Fuck it for a bucket. This one's for you, if you want?'

I knelt down and took a deep lungful, sucking in the smoke until the water touched my lips, then I held my breath.

I felt him squeeze my shoulder.

Did I?

I held my breath.

'You know what I'm talking about,' he said again, quieter now. 'I just mean you can tell me if you want. I tell you—'

I held my breath, and began to replay the conversation I'd over-heard once, when I'd gone into the kitchen and he was talking to his mum, talking about everyday things like what he'd done in school, and how much pain she was in, when she said something else, she said, 'Your brother called earlier. He finds prison so hard Jakey, he finds prison so hard.'

The familiar numbness crept behind my ears, slowing my brain. Fuck it for a bucket. I breathed out, filling the room with smoke.

He wasn't listening. He didn't even look up as I said it, so this made me wonder if perhaps I didn't say anything, if it was just a thought. Except that didn't make sense because it was loud, it was in the room, so maybe he had said it? I was so stoned, that was the problem. But if he said it, surely his lips would have moved? And now I couldn't remember what it was even, what had been said, but the voice was familiar, wasn't it? I was so stoned. I suddenly felt far too stoned.

'Did you hear that?'

'Hear what?' Jacob was holding the flame again, setting up for his turn. 'Hear what?'

'I don't know.'

'Was it my mum?'

'No I fucking didn't.'

'What?'

'What did you just say?'

It was gone again, what did it say? What did it say? I was so stoned.

'What shall we play?'

Jacob switched on the PlayStation 2, and loaded Resident Evil, and I slumped on the floor, staring at the screen, getting lost in the violence, and thought about being a doctor, about making things better, about curing his mum, about curing mine. And there was something else, something else, hidden in a cloud of smoke.

is this question useful?

5	4	3	2	1
very much	*somewhat*	*undecided*	*not really*	*not at all*

I wonder if you believe me? People don't tend to believe me. I've been asked a lot of questions. Questions like:

This voice – his voice – do you hear it inside your head, or does it seem to come from the outside, and what exactly does it say, and does it tell you to do things or just comment on what you're doing already, and have you done any of the things it says, which things, you said your mum takes tablets, what are they for, is anyone else in your family FUCKING MAD, and do you use illicit drugs, how much alcohol do you drink, every week, every day, and how are you feeling in yourself right now, on a scale of 1–10, and what about on a scale of 1–7,400,000,000,000,000,000, 000,000,000, and how is your sleep of late, and what of your appetite, and what exactly did happen that night on the cliff edge, in your own words, do you remember, can you remember, do you have any questions? That sort of thing.

But it doesn't matter how careful I am to think hard, and tell the truth, people don't believe a word I say.

Everything I do is decided for me. There is a plan. I'm not joking. I have a copy of it somewhere. We have meetings, me and some doctors and nurses and anyone else who feels like showing up to take the piss. We have meetings. They're my meetings, so everybody talks about me.

Afterwards I'm given a few sheets of paper, stapled together, with my plan written on them.

It tells me exactly what I have to do with my days, like coming in for therapy groups here at Hope Road Day Centre, and what tablets I should take, and the injections, and who is responsible for what. This is all written down for me. Then there is another plan that comes into play if I don't stick to the first one. It follows me around, like a shadow. This is my life. I'm nineteen years old, and the only thing I have any control over in my entire world is the way I choose to tell this story. So I'm hardly going to fuck about. It would be nice if you'd try to trust me.

the magnolia elephant

In the right light, you can still make out the shadows of Pokémon characters beneath the paint.

Simon's bedroom became a guest room.

It happened over one weekend. 'We should have done this a long time ago,' Dad said.

He was on the stepladder pushing the paint roller. I was working in the corners with a small brush, and Mum was on the landing sorting out piles for Charity Shop and Throw Away. Dad placed the roller down. 'What I mean is—'

'I know what you mean, Dad.'

He was right too. If we'd done it straight away it would have absorbed into the bigger sadness, part of the goodbye. But to hesitate – to wait – it's impossible to know how long to wait. Is a year enough? That becomes two, then three – until half a decade has slipped away, and the elephant in the room is the room itself.

As it happens, I was the one who made the suggestion. This was the Saturday before my granddad was due his second knee operation. With knees they tend to do them one at a time. He'd had the first six months earlier and it had gone okay, but it was hard on Nanny Noo. He was in a wheelchair, then on crutches, and she had to do a lot of lifting and moving him about. Mum and Dad were talking about this over breakfast, about how stubborn she can be, and how much persuading it had taken for her to agree he could stay with us next time. They started laughing about how relieved Granddad had looked when she finally relented. Then I suddenly came out with it, 'Do you think we should redecorate the bedroom for him?'

We shoved heaped spoonfuls of cornflakes into our mouths, and nobody said anything for a bit. We just chewed it over. Mum was the first to swallow. She said, 'Let's do it today.'

In my memory milk squirts out of Dad's nose. But probably it didn't. Memory plays tricks over time. He was shocked though. 'Really, love? I'm sure your dad won't mind if—'

'Let's make it nice for him, okay?'

It's like pulling off a plaster.

No.

It's not like that. It's a far bigger deal. It's only like pulling off a plaster in that once we decided to do it, we did it quickly. I'm not giving lessons in how to grieve. I'm only saying what we did. Dad took measurements of the room with his tape measure, and by early afternoon we were traipsing around B&Q, Allied Carpets, and IKEA.

'Can you bring through more newspaper?' Dad called from the top of the ladder. Mum didn't answer.

'Are you okay, Mum?' She didn't answer me either.

She'd been doing well. In B&Q she'd outright flirted with an assistant for a discount on the rollers, even though they were clearly separate from the Big Sale bucket.

'I'll go,' Dad mouthed to me. He wiped his hands on a paper towel and climbed down the ladder. I stayed in the bedroom, listening.

'Can we change the colour, Richard?'

'You liked it.'

'I know. And I do. Can we?'

I could hear them hugging, a kiss planted on a cheek. 'If we leave now, we'll get there before it closes.'

As they pulled out of the driveway Dad wound down his window, waving and holding his thumb in the air. I took a deep breath, smelling the wet paint. Then I smeared a section with my fingertips and let it dry against my skin. I'm hopeless at naming colours, but it was something like terracotta. It was rich and warm, and all at once I understood they would come back with white or magnolia or one of those colours you see in waiting rooms and offices, but don't really notice.

When we decorate a room, we're wiping away its old personality and giving it a new one. Mum could lose the Pokémon wallpaper and curtains, the aeroplanes on strings. But she didn't want a room people commented on; she didn't want paint with personality. That's what I think, anyway. And it might sound mad, but my mum is mad. We have more in common than we care to admit.

We got rid of my brother's belongings. Even the N64 went to a charity shop, along with three black bin liners full of his clothes. This was Sunday and the shop was closed, so we did what the sign said, and left them in the doorway. That felt strange but we didn't need a ceremony – it was what it was; stuff no longer needed.

Of course his keepsake box stayed. That goes without saying. When everything else was finished, Dad placed it carefully inside the new IKEA wardrobe, and we were done.

I suppose it should have been obvious that after a knee operation my granddad would need a bed downstairs.

Perhaps it was obvious. He stayed with us until he was out of the wheelchair, and all the while he slept on a fold-out in the lounge. As far as I know he never once made it upstairs. He didn't even see the new guest bedroom. Or its magnolia walls.

milestones

It was the way our shadows were cast. The sun was low in the sky behind us, and as I pedalled, my mum kept pace, running three or four steps behind me, shouting encouragement: You're doing it, sweetheart. You're doing it. Looking at the ground, I watched her shadow, watched it slowly recede so that my front wheel was criss-crossing her knees, then torso, then head, and I was pulling away. I really was on my own.

'I'm ready, I can do it.'

'Pardon? I can't hear you.' Mum was calling through my bedroom door. 'Now please. You need to get ready.'

I pushed my face against my mattress, nudging at a spring with my jaw. 'What time is it?'

'It's nearly midday. We need to get going or you'll miss it.'

I took a deep breath. My sheets smelled sweaty and stale. 'I'm not going,' I said.

'Of course you're going.'

'They'll post them.'

'I can't hear you. Can I come in?'

'I said, they'll post them.'

As she opened my door, she gave it a little tap. Then came the sigh, and the smallest shake of her head.

'What? Say it.'

'You're not even up,' she said.

'I'm tired.'

'I thought—'

'I never said I was going.'

In a single movement she picked up clothes from my floor, dropping them into my laundry bin. She stood for a while, looking around the room, noticing the small pipe and bag of that Bloody Stuff on my bedside table, pretending not to notice, and then quickly turning to open my curtains.

'Matthew. What on earth?'

My curtains were no good because the light would creep under the folds, so I'd flattened out empty cereal boxes and taped them over the glass. 'Oh for— what next?'

'Leave it! I need it there. It's too bright.'

'It's meant to be bright, it's called daytime. It's like a cave in here.'

'I mean it. Leave it.'

She stared at the cardboard, her hand still raised to take it down. Then she closed the curtains again. Turning to face me, planting her hands on her hips, 'If you're out of your deodorant, you know you can just put it on the list don't you? I can't keep track of what everyone needs all the time. It's what the list is for.'

'What are you talking about? Who said anything about—'

'It's just a bit stuffy in here. And I don't mind getting you Lynx or whichever it is you want, but you need to put it on the list because—'

'Jesus. I didn't ask you to come in.'

'No. But what if a friend came around?'

'Like who?'

'Like, like anyone. Like Jacob. It's not the point. Now please, for me. Please Matt. Even if you don't care how you've done, I still do.'

In life there are milestones. Events that mark out certain days as being special from the other days.

They begin before we're old enough to know about them, like the day we uttered our first proper word, and the day we took our first steps. We made it through the night without a nappy. We learnt other people have feelings, and the stabilizers came off our bikes.

If we're lucky – and I am, I do know that – we get help along the way. Nobody swam my first width of the pool for me, but Dad drove me back and forth to swimming classes, even though he'd never learnt to swim himself, and when I got awarded my Tony the Tiger Five Metres badge, it was Mum who carefully sewed it onto my swimming trunks. So I reckon a lot of my early milestones were their milestones too.

Mum's hands slipped from her hips, then she folded her arms across her chest, then back to her hips.

She was nervous – that was it.

'Even if you don't care how you've done, I still do.'

She'd woken up first thing with my dad and driven him to work. In the car they'd listened to the radio. I can't know this. I'm guessing. It's what you might call an educated guess. On the local news a roaming reporter had based himself at one of the high schools. They didn't catch which one, but maybe mine. The reporter talked about how average GCSE grades were up for the millionth year in a row; he talked about how boys were closing the gap on girls; he talked about a slight increase in home education, and Mum felt her tummy do a somersault. Then he took his regional accent to meet a group of squealing girls – prising one away for the obligatory interview. Um, four A stars, 3 As and two Bs, the girl says, breathless with excitement. Oh, and a C in Maths, she giggles. I hate Maths.

Getting out of the car, Dad paused. 'He's a smart lad. He'll have done okay.'

Mum answered quietly. 'Yes. I know.'

I'm guessing. It's an educated guess.

Sitting in slow traffic, in slight drizzle – enough to use the windscreen wipers, but not enough to stop them squeaking – Mum would have allowed herself the small luxury of imagining the perfect morning.

In this morning, this perfect morning, she'd get home and I'd be out of bed already – waiting for her in the kitchen. I've made myself some toast but hardly taken a bite. I'm too nervous. 'Do you mind driving me Mum? It's just— I want you to be there.'

'Of course,' she smiles. She sits beside me at the table, stealing a cheeky bite of toast. 'Now listen,' she says.

Now listen.

Listen.

Listen.

Sitting in traffic, she rehearsed.

Her voice would be perfect. A soothing voice – tender and reassuring. Not her scratchy, knotted voice. Not the exasperated I'll-count-to-ten-and-start-again voice, the voice I'd started mimicking to send her over the edge.

'Now listen. You have nothing to be nervous about. You worked so hard. You tried your best. And really, Matt. That's all that matters.'

Then the doubts appeared. Or they were there all along, but now she noticed them. Like specks of rain on the windscreen. The way you can look right through them at first, focus into the distance, as if they're not even there, but as soon as you see them, you can't stop seeing them. For this perfect morning, there would have needed to be other perfect mornings: a string of days before this, where I actually had worked hard, when I had tried my best.

And by now – I'm guessing, I'm only guessing – the car in front had long since pulled away, and the driver behind beeped his horn. Mum panicked and stalled the engine.

By the time she got home, she had already worked herself into a state – was already weighing up the decision to wake me and drive me in, or take a yellow pill and head back to bed herself.

'I'm not going,' I said again. The bed spring twanged against my jaw. 'You don't have to collect them. It says in the letter. If you don't show up they post them.'

'But— It doesn't make sense. Please. I'll drive you.'

'No. I'm not going.'

Mum had her own theories. They filled the dark space at the foot of my bed.

'Do you want to hurt me?' she asked.

I rolled over, end of the conversation.

I didn't hear her leave.

I lifted from my saddle, pushing harder on the pedals. Pulling at the handlebars. It was there in the distance. Far in the distance, but getting closer with each turn of the wheels.

It erupted from the ground and reached high into the sky – glass and bricks and concrete.

I watched my front wheel, watched it criss-cross her knees, her torso, her head. I was pulling away.

I'm doing it. I'm really doing it.

You know what dreams are like.

the same story

Only fifteen minutes today, then puncture time. I have a few compliance problems with tablets, the answer – a long, sharp needle.

Every other week, alternate sides.

I'd rather not think about it now. It's best not to think until the injection is actually going in.

Fuck this.

I'm going home.

MAKE YOURSELF AT HOME

I didn't tell you where I live yet.

It probably doesn't matter, but I'll tell you now, because then you can have some pictures in your mind as you read. Reading is a bit like hallucinating.

Hallucinate this:

An ash grey sky over a block of council flats, painted jaundice yellow. I'll buzz you up. It's the sixth floor, No. 607. Come in. The narrow, dim-lit hall is cluttered with pairs of old trainers, empty Coke and Dr Pepper bottles, takeaway menus, and free newspapers.

To your left is the kitchen, sorry about the mess. The kettle's billowing steam onto the peeling lime green wallpaper. There is an ashtray by the window, and if you open those blinds you can spy on half of Bristol.

It can spy on you too.

The toilet's just across the hall but the bolt doesn't slide properly, so you'll need to prop it closed with a doorstop. On the ceiling is the carcass of a spider, tangled in its own web. My razor blade is getting blunt, and I'm out of toothpaste.

I have a small bedroom with a single mattress on the floor, and a Hungarian Goose Down Pillow bought from John Lewis for nearly fifty pounds. The room smells of broken sleep and marijuana, and well into the night you can hear my neighbours bickering above your head.

In the main room a couple of rugs cover a worn-through carpet. I spend most of my time in here and do try to keep it tidy, but it's small so feels cluttered whatever. I do not have a television or a radio. On the small wooden table beside the window is a book called Living with Voices, and a few loose stacks of my writing and sketches.

In the far corner, and stretching across the back wall behind the armchair and curtains, is the tangled mass of sprawling plastic tubing and dirt-encrusted bottles and jars, that make up what has survived of my Special Project.

Today it's warm because I've had the heating on. I don't usually bother, but I did today because it's Thursday, which means Nanny Noo has been to visit me. To be honest, I didn't want her to come because I was worried she might slip on the ice. There has been so much snow lately, more than I've ever seen, and where it is starting to melt away, the crisp white has turned to a dirty slush.

I don't own a phone, so first thing this morning I threw some stuff in a carrier bag for The Pig, put on my coat and set off to the public payphone at the end of the street. I dialled Nanny Noo's number.

'4960216.' That's how my granddad answers the telephone. He answers by telling you what you have just dialled. It's pointless.

'Granddad, it's Matthew.'

'Hello?' My granddad has bad hearing, so you have to speak loudly on the phone to him.

'IT'S MATTHEW.'

'Matthew, your nan's on her way.'

'I didn't want her to come, because of the ice.'

'I told her not to go because of the ice, but she's stubborn.'

'Okay Granddad. Bye.'

'Hello?'

'BYE GRANDDAD.'

'Your nanny's on her way. She just left.'

I didn't go straight back. I walked to the mini market and bought two potatoes and a can of Carlsberg Special Brew.

I don't know if you've been to Bristol, but if you have then you might know that triangle of grass and broken glass where Jamaica Street joins Cheltenham Road - just along from the homeless hostel and The

Massage Parlour where they charge for full sex even if you only want cuddles and breast feeding. There are usually a few homeless people hanging about, killing time. I like The Pig most.

That's an unkind name, but it's what he calls himself. He does look like a pig too. His nostrils are turned up in a snout, and he has piggy little eyes behind thick dirty lenses. He even snorts. To be honest, he plays it up a bit.

We never really met, so much as kept bumping into each other. Each morning when I walk to the Day Centre, and each afternoon when I come back home, he's always there. I wouldn't usually make a special point of seeing him, but last night I kept imagining being homeless in this weather. It's easier to sleep with problems if you know you're going to do something about them. So I decided this morning I'd take him a couple of jumpers and a flask of Chicken & Mushroom Cup-a-Soup.

'Okay Lad?' He always calls me Lad. I think he probably can't remember my name. We're not close friends, we just sit together sometimes.

'Alright, The Pig. Cold innit?'

I opened my Special Brew. The Pig is an alcoholic, so I feel a bit guilty when I drink with him. He shook his Big Issue at a woman wearing fluffy snow boots. She smiled politely, and crossed the road.

He doesn't actually sell the Big Issue. He waves one around from time to time to get attention, and if someone wants to buy it he asks if they could give him money instead. I keep meaning to get him the latest copy. The other week this guy with ginger dreadlocks and a duffel coat lectured him for giving legitimate vendors a bad name. He actually stopped in the street just to tell him off. Then he offered about eight pence in coppers, and bounced across the street to a bar. I suppose he had a point. But he was still a wanker.

I gulped back the last of my can. It doesn't taste too nice; it's more a functional drink.

'You forgot your bag, Lad.'

'No. That's for you.'

He opened the flask, sniffing the soup like a pig after truffles. He might have been hoping for something stronger.

As I cut back through the empty garages and up the footpath, Nanny Noo was rounding the corner in her car. She waved in that sudden nervous way people do when they aren't expecting to see you, or if they're afraid to take their hand off the steering wheel. I waited for her to park, and helped her out.

'I didn't want you to come, because of the ice.'

'Nonsense. Help me with these bags.'

She is very generous. I told you that. And whenever she visits she brings me some food for our lunch, and extra for me to have in the week, and a bottle or two of fizzy pop. That's what she calls it. Fizzy pop.

'That one too,' she said, pointing at a cream-coloured plastic case with a brown handle.

'What is it?'

'It's heavy. Can you manage it?'

'Yes. What's in it?'

'Wait and see.'

The lift is out-of-order. It's always out-of-order, and even when it isn't there's usually another reason you might not want your Nanny Noo to use it, like if someone has taken a piss in the corner, or graffitied something cruel about you. I've lived here more than two years now, since I was seventeen, and I'm not sure Nanny has ever once used the lift. I worry about her falling on the stairs though, so I walked up behind her. She calls me a gentleman.

'Look at this mess.'

'Sorry Nanny. I meant to clean up.'

Seventeen was still young to leave home, I know that. And I probably wouldn't have had the guts to move out on my own, but I wasn't on my own, not at the beginning. I should talk about that in a bit.

In the kitchen we placed the bags of food out on the counter. 'I already bought potatoes,' I offered. 'I thought I'd make us jacket potatoes.'

I was feeling light-headed from the drink, and I

hoped it would be a short visit. I can be selfish like that.

'Good boy. But no. You'll starve. I'll make us a pasta bake.'

With Nanny Noo it is best not to protest too much. She can be very stubborn. So I loitered around and helped her slice vegetables. The good thing with Nanny Noo is that she doesn't talk much, and she doesn't ask many questions.

'Have you seen your mum recently?'

Except that one, she did ask that one. I didn't answer her though. Nanny Noo smiled and put her hand on mine. 'You're a good boy Matthew, we just worry about you.'

'Who does?'

'I do. And your mum, and your father. But they might worry less if you saw them more often.' She squeezed my fingers, and I thought about how her hand is a lot like my mum's; cold, with papery flesh.

'How's Granddad?' I asked

'Getting old, Matthew. We're both getting old.'

I hope she never dies.

So we ate pasta bake. I sat on the wooden chair and she sat on the armchair with the busy floral pattern and the soft cushions. She ran her fingernails over the blistered part on the arm where I sometimes put out cigarettes, and she started to form a thought about how I needed to be more careful. Then she looked at

what's left of my Special Project - the remaining jars
and tubes that I can't ever seem to bring myself to
throw away, even after so long. She started to form
a thought about that too, but then what she actually
said was, 'It's nice to see you, Matthew.'

'Thanks. I'll clean up next time.'

She smiled and rubbed her hands together, saying,
'Do you want your present then?'

'You got me something?'

I'd left the plastic case in the hall so went to get
it, and placed it on the carpet in front of Nanny Noo.
'Open it up then,' she said.

'What is it?'

'Well, open it and see. You push those clips at the
side.'

I suppose it's an unusual gift to buy someone these
days, but Nanny saw it in a charity shop and she
thought of me. 'For your writing,' she said.

It was probably the Special Brew, but I felt so
happy I could have cried.

'Well, it isn't a computer,' she said. 'I know that.
But these are what we used to type on when I was your
age, and they were good enough. There's a bit of a knack
to it. If you tap more than one key at a time those
arms tend to get jammed, and there isn't a delete, but,
well, I thought it might be useful for writing your
stories.'

It's hard to know what to say sometimes, when someone does something so nice. It's hard to know where to look.

We took our dishes through to the kitchen and I started the washing up, and Nanny Noo took her secret pack of menthol cigarettes out of the drawer. I'm the only person in the family who knows that she smokes, and she only smokes with me. I'm not saying that to show off because it's a stupid thing to show off about. But it does make me feel important, somehow. I can't explain it.

She blew smoke out of the window and said, 'Horrid day, isn't it?'

'No. It's a good day,' I answered, washing a smudge of ink from my thumb. 'It's a really good day.'

She didn't stay much longer. We walked down the stairwell, with her arm through mine. Then before she climbed into her car she kissed me twice; once on the forehead, once on the cheek. I smoked another cigarette by the big yellow bins, and watched one of my neighbours kick his dog.

Anyway, I just thought I should say where I live. It isn't perfect, but it's home, and now that I have a typewriter, I'm not leaving any time soon.

Matthew Homes
Flat 607
Terrence House
Kingsdown
Bristol

Friday 5th Feb '10

Dear Matthew,

I popped by to check if everything is okay. You disappeared from Hope Road very suddenly on Wednesday, and we didn't see you today either? I'll be on duty until 5 p.m, but will keep my work mobile with me this evening too, so when you get this give me a call if you can on 07700 900934 (I've put 50p in the envelope because I know you don't always have change for the phone).

All the best,
Denise Lovell
Care Co-ordinator
Brunel CMHT - Bristol

SHE DIDN'T MENTION THE NEEDLE. You'll notice she didn't mention that. Popping by to check if everything is okay? Yeah, right. And if I did answer the door it would be, Oh whilst I'm here Matt we might as well give you your injection too.

No thanks.

Not today Denise Lovell. I'm busy telling my story, thank you.

She stayed at the door for ages too. Standing there, knocking, standing there, knock knock knock. It must have been ten minutes at least, with me being careful not to make a sound, before she finally gave up and pushed the note through the letter box.

I need to be careful though. I am a mentally unwell man, and things have gone wrong for me before.

RELAPSE INDICATORS

1. Voice: No.

2. Atoms: No.

3. Not engaging with support team: Oops.

Two out of three ain't bad.

It was Jacob Greening's idea that we should leave home after Year 11, and rent a place together. Our own flat, he said. It'll be wicked. I thought so too. It was so easy to imagine the two of us together, forever.

Am I rushing?

The first thing we had to do was get jobs, which wasn't difficult because we didn't mind what we did. He found his at a 24-Hour Kebab House. Then I had my interview for care assistant work at a home for the elderly. The manager asked if I had any experience of care work, and I said that I did because I helped to look after a disabled person, so I knew about bedsores and Sudocrem and hoists and mouth care and bed baths and commodes and catheters and slide sheets and Fortisips and that kind of thing, and that I enjoyed it.

The manager smiled, and asked if I was happy to work night shifts.

Yes.

It's enough to drive you crazy, Mum said. It's like talking to a brick wall, she said. She went on and on about A Levels, about college. About how well I did in my GCSEs even though I didn't try, even though I refused to quit smoking that BLOODY STUFF.

She talked about my potential.

I've never understood what is so special about achieving potential. In the care home I got to learn about the different residents. I knew more about them than they did. Each resident had a folder that was kept in a locked drawer beside their bed. In the front, stuck with Sellotape to the inside cover was a short note, written by the resident. Except it wasn't really written by them because half of them were too demented to know what a pen was. It was just made to look as if they had written it, to make it more personal.

It might say,

HELLO, my name is Sylvia Stevens. I prefer to be called Mrs Stevens please. I used to work as a secretary and I am very proud of my five beautiful grandchildren. I need to have my food cut up for me but I prefer to eat it by myself so please be patient if this takes me a while. At night-time I like to listen to Radio 4. This helps me sleep.

Or it might say,

HELLO, my name is Terry Archibald. You can call me Terry. I was a merchant seaman and historian. I even wrote a history book which you can find in the manager's office. Please be careful with it because there are not many copies left. I get confused sometimes, and can hit out if I feel threatened so please keep talking to me to keep me calm when you are doing my personal care. My wife visits on Wednesdays and Sundays.

Or it might say,

HELLO, my name is William Roberts. Most people call me Bill. I have committed several horrendous sex crimes against young girls, including both of my daughters, for which I have never been brought to justice. Please liquidize my food and feed it to me. I am allowed a small beaker of Stout near bedtime.

Or,

HELLO, my name is your potential. But you can call me impossible. I am the missed opportunities. I am the expectations you will never fulfil. I am always taunting you, regardless of how hard you try, regardless of how much you hope. Please put talcum powder on my arse when you wash me, and take note of how our shit smells exactly the same.

Ignore me. I'm just pissed off today. Who does Denise
Lovell think she is, coming to my home, trying to catch
me out? Why can't they just leave me alone?

Ignore me.

YOU'RE AN ASSET TO THE TEAM, the manager would say.

I was always first to volunteer covering shifts when staff went off sick. And I'd never complain when he put my name down for extra night duty. I don't know how we coped without you, he would say.

I'd get an hour's break at three o'clock in the morning, to have some sleep before getting breakfast ready for the residents. I didn't go to sleep. I used to get on my bike and ride through the silent streets to the park, to our bench beside the tree. Sometimes Jacob would be there first, waiting for me, or sometimes I would get there first and watch him come speeding through the top entrance, across the path and onto the grass, cycling so fast that his bike juddered and rattled, until he was right beside the bench where he'd slam on his brake and kick the back wheel out in a skid, churning up the damp earth.

He would bring us cheeseburgers and chips from the

Kebab House, and we would spend our break together, looking at the night, eating junk, talking about our plan to rent a flat as soon as we had enough cash saved up. This flat, our flat, our life. It was all so easy.

BUT WE CAN HELP, Mum offered, hovering nervously in the driveway.

She hadn't slept all night. I had heard her rummaging in the attic for old sets of crockery and cutlery and the kettle and toaster that they'd been bought as wedding presents, kept in dusty boxes. She was sort of whimpering as she did it. Eventually I'd heard my dad say, 'That's enough, love. Come to bed. It's really late.'

Now we were surrounded by the first chapter of my life, neatly packed away.

'Your dad will be home in a couple of hours,' she said. 'We can take a few car loads. Please, let us help.'

'I'm okay. We've got it sorted.'

Jacob had made friends with this guy from the Kebab House. Hamed, I think his name was. He was the owner's son or something. He was a couple of years older than us and drove his own van, which had lowered suspension

and stick-on blacked-out windows, and half the space
in the back was taken up with a sound system that made
the whole ground vibrate as he pulled up beside us.

He threw a cigarette butt into the gutter and reached
to shake Mum's hand through the open window. 'So your
big boy is flying the nest, is it?'

Mum glared at him.

Hamed rubbed the back of his neck and squinted at
the sky. 'Good day for it, innit.'

If I think about it now, there was a lot of stuff that
Jacob never bothered to pack. Things like his posters,
things like his winter clothes.

Mrs Greening had been encouraging from the start.
'You need your own life Jakey,' she'd said. 'I'm so proud
of you two boys.' Her voice was all trembly though, it
was obvious she was frightened. Care in the Community
had been stepping up their support, but Jacob still did
so much.

She had this plastic gripper that she would clip
onto pens and pencils to make them fatter and easier
for her to hold. It must have taken her ages to make
the card. It had this picture of a house, the way a
child might draw a house, with smoke coming out of the
chimney, fluffy clouds in the sky, the sun coloured
in yellow, with this big wonky smile on its face. She
was embarrassed by the picture because she knew I was

good at art. That's what she said as she gave it to us. And she said she was sorry it didn't have an envelope, and that we obviously didn't have to put it on display.

'It's brilliant,' I said.

I meant it too. It reminded me of something. I couldn't place it at the time, but it made me feel happy and sad all at once.

At the flat Jacob would stick it onto the fridge with his bottle opener fridge magnet. CONGRATULATIONS ON YOUR NEW HOME. But for now it was propped on the dashboard of the van, and he was staring at it and not saying a word. It wasn't only his mum who was frightened. He was too.

I reckon my mum had to fight the urge to climb into a cardboard box, hoping I'd pack her neatly away at the other end.

'There's no shame in coming home if it doesn't work out.'

She didn't say that quietly. She made sure it was loud enough for Jacob to hear too, even over the music.

'It will work out,' I snapped, glaring at her.

I blew her a Goodbye and Good Fucking Riddance kiss. It was cruel of me, but she couldn't read the small print. She did that thing where you pretend to catch it and press it against your heart.

These are the moments that make the dot-to-dot

pictures of our past; everything else is simply filling
in the gaps.

We blasted at the horn, swerving wildly.

The little boy appeared from nowhere, running into
the road, cutting through traffic.

He wore a big orange coat, and I didn't make out his
face because his hood was pulled right up. But I think,
I think, in that moment, he was me. I had tried to run
away, but Mum caught me by the school. She carried me
to the doctor's, and I could hear her heartbeat through
my stupid hood.

Looking in the wing mirror, I expected to see her
chasing.

Baby, wait. Please.

No.

She hadn't moved. She stood perfectly still, with my
kiss held against her. She would stay that way until
my dad arrived home from work, when he would take her
inside, and fetch her a tablet.

Goodbye, and

Good Fucking Riddance.

THE FIRST EVENING, neither of us had to work.

We didn't have proper furniture, so we placed our single mattresses side by side on the bedroom floor, and sat on them. We took the light bulb from the hall because it was the only one the previous tenants had left behind. And I plugged my old desk lamp in the kitchen, so we could see to cook.

We ate oven chips with baked beans and lots of tomato ketchup, and shared a 3-litre bottle of cider.

I've made it sound shit. It wasn't. It was perfect.

The second evening, we both had to work.

So at three o'clock in the morning we rode our bikes to our bench beside the tree and watched night turn to twilight.

Jacob talked about crepuscular animals. It was a new word he'd learnt, and he was showing off. He said that him and me were crepuscular because we mostly lived in dusk and dawn. He gets excited by the unlikeliest things. It can make people feel uncomfortable. Jacob is one of those people who other people share whispered comments about. They say things like, 'He struggles in his own skin, doesn't he?' And the other people shake their heads thoughtfully, and say, 'There is something, isn't there?'

'You're my best mate, Jacob.'

'I should fucking hope so.'

I felt his fingers brush against mine. Not quite holding hands, not quite not holding hands. Each of us gripping at the bench slats.

The third evening, I was home by myself.

I had a shower before bed. As I dried, I caught sight of myself in the steamed-up bathroom mirror.

Ha.

You don't know what I look like.

I only just thought that. I haven't once said what I look like. I did say that I'm tall and getting fat. I did say that much, but you might not have remembered. Getting fat is a common side effect of my medication.

Denise Lovell gave me a Patient Information Sheet, with them all listed in microscopic letters.

COMMON SIDE EFFECTS, it says:

anxiety;	increased saliva production;
sleepiness;	appetite changes;
blurred vision;	restlessness;
shaking or tremor;	light-headedness;
sweating;	rash;
nausea;	stomach pain or upset;
dizziness;	pain at the injection site;
depression;	fatigue;
headache;	trouble sleeping;
vomiting;	weight gain.

Happy days, eh? You don't want to know about the less common ones.

Nah, fuck it. Why not:

Severe allergic reactions; infections; abnormal thoughts; abnormal gait; itching; drooling; mask-like facial expression; fever; severe anxiety; sexual dysfunction; convulsions; suicidal thoughts or attempts; breathing difficulties; irregular heartbeat; trouble concentrating, speaking, or swallowing; trouble sitting still; trouble standing or walking; muscle spasms; seizures; nightmares; killing your own brother, again.

I'm getting ahead of myself.

I wasn't on the fucking stuff yet. In the bathroom mirror were the blurred edges of a healthy young man

with a new job, a new home, and the promise of a whole
new life. I should have wiped away the condensation
and taken a proper look at him.

I wish I'd done that now.

But I didn't, so you can't either.

Matthew Homes
Flat 607
Terrence House
Kingsdown
Bristol

Mon 8th Feb '10

Dear Matthew,

I'm a bit concerned about you. I was hoping you might have got in touch with the team over the weekend but we didn't hear anything. And we didn't see you at the day centre again today.

I know you don't like us to make a fuss Matt, and I respect that, but we do need to stay in contact. And it's still very important you have your depot injection. This is what you agreed to in your Community Treatment Order. We can talk about this.

Please give me a call on 07700 900934 or ring the office on 0117 496 0777 as soon as possible. Hope you had a nice weekend, anyway?

Kind Regards,
Denise Lovell
Care Co-ordinator
Brunel CMHT - Bristol

P.S. I've filled out my part of the new DLA forms too, so perhaps we can go through those together. I think you might even be entitled to a bit more money!

KNOCK KNOCK KNOCK knock knock knock knock. She was
there for ten minutes again, propping open the letter
box, peering through. Knock knock knock. Hello, Matt.
Are you home? Knock KNOCK KNOCK.

I could feel her breath.

She didn't see me though because I was sitting down
here, with my back to the door, keeping a close ear on
things. Since you ask Denise Lovell, no I did not have a
nice weekend. I've been feeling a bit sorry for myself
as it happens.

Nanny Noo tells me off for that. She says it doesn't
help to dwell, how it's important to be grateful for
the everyday things, that there's happiness in a cooked
meal or a stroll in the fresh air. I know she's right
too. Except it's easier to find happiness in a cooked
meal when there's somebody else to pass you the ketchup.
For all our plans together Jacob didn't live with me
for very long. Perhaps four or five months.

We never had a Christmas here together, we didn't reach our eighteenth birthdays. I know it's stupid to care too much about stuff like that. It's my own fault anyway.

I should write about why he left.

But there are different versions of truth. If we meet each other in the street, glance away and look back, we might look the same, feel the same, think the same, but the subatomic particles, the smallest parts of us that make every other part, will have rushed away, been replaced at impossible speeds. We will be completely different people. Everything changes all the time.

Truth changes.

Here are three truths.

Knock

KNOCKKNOCK

Truth No. 1

I didn't have my armchair yet. The main room seemed bigger without it, and he looked small, crouched on the carpet in the dusty light beneath the window. He buried his face in his hands. I couldn't say how long he'd been there, but I think for a long time.

I'd been sleeping after a night shift and was still holding my expensive pillow. It was a gift from John Lewis that Nanny Noo and Granddad bought me, to help with my bad dreams; the dreams that had started to follow me outside of sleep, so that sometimes I would have to cut a little at my skin with a knife, or burn myself with a lighter, to make sure I was real.

I can't speak for Jacob, but when I think about things now, there was more to it than his mum; I was becoming a problem.

We didn't talk straight away. The only noise was the faraway sound of traffic, drifting through the window. You can hear it all the time, but only notice it when there is a silence that needs filling.

I wasn't sure he'd seen me, until after a while he said, 'She was slumped forwards in her chair again, with the neck rest too high up.'

'We can say something.'

'It's more than that.'

They sent different people round, that was a problem. Each morning it could be a new carer getting her up. Nobody knew Mrs Greening properly, or the way things had to be done.

'It was her hair,' he said.

I've replayed the conversation in my head so many times. I imagine myself saying different things, then what he would say differently. I move the memory around the flat like it's a piece of furniture, or a picture in a frame that I can't decide where to hang.

'What are those things, like little girls have?'

'What?'

'In their hair.'

'I don't know. Pigtails, is it?'

'Yeah, them.'

I used to brush Mrs Greening's hair, whilst Jacob prepared her tea and got her medicine ready. I'd wash it sometimes too. She had this special sink, like you see in hairdressers but with padded bits that fold over the edges. She didn't have much feeling in her arms and legs, but her head felt tingly and nice when I rubbed in the shampoo. That's what she said, anyway. And she said I was better at it than Jacob because he pulled too hard, but I wasn't to tell him because we were both her angels.

'What are you smiling for?'

'I'm not.'

'It's not fucking funny, Matt.'

'I wasn't smiling about-'

'I bet you're exactly the same. In that old people's home, you probably treat them like fucking children too.'

He didn't mean that, but it still hurt.

'No I don't. You know I wouldn't-'

'Well quit fucking smiling then. She was there trying to pull the things out all morning. But the more wound up she is, the worse her hands get. Now these three fingers-'

His voice trailed away. He didn't cry, I've never seen him cry. But I think he was close. 'These three fingers, they don't really work at all.'

I dropped my pillow on the carpet and sat beside him. The acne that had clung to his face all through school was finally clearing away. He'd started growing a beard too. Except it didn't reach his sideburns, so there were these two lopsided islands of soft pink at the top of his cheeks.

He smelled like he always smelled: Lynx deodorant and cooking fat from the Kebab House.

'I don't know what to say, Jacob.'

He sniffed and wiped at his nose with the back of his sleeve. 'You don't get it,' he said softly. 'She's all on her own.'

It was a strange moment. Not because of what he said, but the way he looked at me. He'd looked at me like that once before. This was a long time ago but it was the exact same look. I knew what I had to do, except I didn't want to. So I replay the memory a different way.

Truth No. 2

I place us in the kitchen, and because I don't want to
say anything that will make it worse, I swill out dirty
mugs to make tea. Problems seem less if we have them
with a cup of tea, that's another thing Nanny Noo says.

I noticed the CONGRATULATIONS ON YOUR NEW HOME
card Mrs Greening had made, still stuck to the fridge
door, spotted in fat from all the frying we did. When
she gave it to us I didn't understand the feeling it
gave me.

Now I did.

For my brother's tenth birthday our mum arranged a
huge party. It was in our local Beavers and Brownies
Hut, decorated with balloons and banners. On a long
table at the far end were bowls of Hula Hoops, biscuits,
and sausages on sticks. There was pineapple and cheese
on sticks too, except one of Simon's friends got to them
first and bit off all the pineapple chunks so they
were just cheese.

Loads of people came because Simon was allowed
friends from his school and I was even allowed some
from mine.

Nanny Noo and Granddad were there, and Aunty Mel who
came all the way from Manchester with Uncle Brian and

our three cousins, and my other aunt, Jacqueline, who
lives much closer, but who we didn't often see because
her and Mum don't get on, and because she dresses all in
black and talks too much about magic and spirits, and
will never not smoke even at children's parties.

We played a game where we had to put on a hat and a
scarf and thick woollen mittens, then try to eat a bar
of Dairy Milk with a knife and fork. But the most fun
was at the end when we ran around the hall stamping
on the balloons, making them pop.

Simon called it his best birthday ever.

I made him a card, and you have to remember I was
still only little. What I'd done was draw a house with
a smiling sunshine over the top, exactly like Mrs
Greening had done, but what made it good was that I'd
put diagonal lines coming off the house so that instead
of being a flat square, it looked three-dimensional.
Nobody had told me how either, I'd worked it out by
myself.

It was just one of a hundred cards he was given, and
for ages Mum let him keep them up around the living
room, cluttering the mantelpiece and the coffee table.
I didn't know if he liked mine, or had even noticed it.
Until the day Mum said they had to come down.

She was in a bad mood and had been telling me off
for the mess my room was in, how I made her life a
bloody uphill struggle, she couldn't wait until the

holidays were over and I was out from under her feet.

I was probably too sensitive because it's normal for mums to lose their temper once in a while, especially during summer holidays with two boys causing havoc. It isn't like she ever hit us or anything, so I know I was too sensitive. By the time her attention spilled to the cards and Simon got his turn, I was whimpering like a baby.

Simon marched straight up to the windowsill and took down my card. He scrunched his face and bit at his tongue in the way he did when he was concentrating. Then he told me that I should be a professional. Except he couldn't say professional properly and had to try about six times to get the word out. He asked me to show him how I did it, and we spent the afternoon sitting at the kitchen table, drawing pictures together. I told him that he should be a professional too.

He shook his head and looked away.

The card I made him was the only one to make it into his stupid keepsake box, and when I found it there after he died, and when I think about it now, I'm happy and sad all at once.

Jacob was leaning against the counter. Perhaps he felt the same as me, for all his own reasons. But what came out of him was anger. I dropped teabags into the mugs and filled the kettle. He didn't need me to say anything. He could be angry all by himself.

'She wouldn't even talk about it. She asked me to take them out and not to talk about it.'

I took the milk from the fridge and poured some into one of the mugs. Jacob is one of those people who likes the milk and sugar in first. As the water began to boil, he did too.

'Who does that? Who puts a fucking grown adult's hair like that? Like she's a little girl. Like she's their fucking doll.'

My mind was snatched away.

I was distracted by the connections, I'd find them everywhere, because we're all made of the same stuff, the same interstellar dust; a little girl and a doll, the salt in the air, the rain soaking through my clothes. He is begging me, Stop. Stop. Stop. His trembling hands are clutching the torch. He tries to run, his stupid way of running, hunched right forwards with his legs wide apart. She wants to play with you, Simon. She wants to play chase.

Jacob slammed his fist hard on the surface, rattling stacks of dirty plates, sending cutlery clattering onto the greasy lino. 'You ain't listening. You never listen.'

'I am–'

'What's the matter with you?'

'Nothing.'

'Well fucking listen to me then.'

'I'm sorry–'

'She won't say anything because she's too embarrassed, or she's scared she'll embarrass them. Like they give a shit. She just sits there, staring at the wall, staring out the fucking window whilst they do whatever they want.'

He stopped as abruptly as he'd started.

I wanted to shake him. I wanted to shout that he couldn't stay at home with her forever, that it was his idea we lived together in the first place. He couldn't abandon me now.

I didn't do that though. I listened to the kettle boil. I watched steam turn to water droplets on the wallpaper. I could feel Jacob looking at me, and I remembered him looking that way once before.

Truth No. 3

He didn't say much at all.

He isn't the sort to talk about stuff, not the important things like mothers and brothers and the way we feel inside. You won't find Jacob Greening hunched over a typewriter, staining paper with his family secrets.

We were in my bedroom. We put on a CD for a bit, and I can't remember what we listened to, only that it kept skipping and that he turned it off. We were stoned, I know that.

He'd been getting us some decent green from that Hamed guy, and we had upgraded from our home-made Buckets to a tall glass Bong we bought from St Nick's market as a sort of moving-in present.

I don't smoke much any more, but at the time I was easily getting through half an ounce a week. Denise Lovell reckons that was a big part of the problem. When I told her about the designs I used to draw, how it felt like my hand was being moved for me, she said that I was probably fucking mental already, it was just that nobody knew it yet.

Jacob was background noise. There was something about his mum, the way they'd done her hair.

He was holding my pillow, hugging it.

I had my sketch pad open in front of me and was watching the pen scratch across the page.

It was happening so fast, I didn't know what I was drawing. Only that it was taking shape exactly as it was meant to. In the middle was a box, not flat to the page, but in three dimensions, like a card I had drawn for Simon years before.

'Stop it.'

And stretching out around it like tentacles were a series of tubes, each connecting to smaller boxes. Not boxes, cylinders.

'For fuck's sake, what are you doing?'

They formed a ring around the centre. In turn, more tubes connected these to each other, and again outwards, to a second ring of cylinders and a third.

He snatched the pad away, 'It's fucking stupid, stop doing it.'

It wasn't only that page. I'd drawn it over and over. I might have been drawing it for days.

Jacob tore them up, ripping each sheet into tiny pieces.

'They were mine,' I said.

'You're losing the plot, man.'

'That was my last sketch pad.'

'Then do something different. Play XBox with me.'

I stood up and walked over to the far wall. It wasn't

like I was moving the pen myself, it was like I was watching it happen.

'We'll lose our deposit,' he pleaded.

'I'm not going anywhere.'

'Please—'

'What? What do you want? I'm busy! You can see I'm fucking busy!'

I shouted at him. I didn't mean to, but my voice tore out of me. He looked afraid, and suddenly I felt ashamed. I turned back to the wall and watched another cylinder take shape in front of me. 'I'm sorry. I'm busy that's all, you can see I'm busy. I have to do this, right.'

The sound of faraway traffic drifted through the open window, and another sound too. I couldn't make it out. Jacob smoked two cigarettes before he spoke another word.

'Remember at school,' he said at last. He spoke so quietly, like he was afraid the memory might hear him and run away. 'Remember the first day, when you loaned me your tie?'

I felt my pen drop to the carpet. 'That was a long time ago, wasn't it?'

'Yeah. I'll never forget.'

I had given him my tie and he wrapped it inside his collar. Then he turned to me, helplessly.

I didn't need to see him now. I knew he was looking

at me in the exact same way. I move the memory around like it's a piece of furniture, but it always ends up here. He didn't only need to borrow my tie. He needed me to tie it up.

We are selfish, my illness and I. We think only of ourselves. We shape the world around us into messages, into secret whispers spoken only for us.

I did one last thing for someone else.

'It's okay,' I said. 'I understand.'

Jacob couldn't stay, it wasn't fair to make him.

'I'm sorry, Matt.'

I didn't cry. He's never seen me cry. But I was close. 'You should look after your mum,' I said. 'She needs you.'

I tied us up neatly for Jacob. I gave him my permission to leave. He said we'd still hang out all the time.

I suppose that makes us friends.

Knock
KNOCKKNOCK

THERE IS A DEAD BIRD. It's on the ground beside the yellow bins, and it's making me feel a bit messed up.

I didn't notice it to begin with because I was keeping a lookout in case Denise rounded the corner in her car and I had to run back inside. I'm out of tobacco so I was smoking one of Nanny Noo's secret menthol cigarettes, and I only noticed the dead bird when I threw the butt onto the ground and went to stamp on it.

It's a chick. I don't know what sort, but it's really small and it doesn't have any feathers or even eyes. It's in a patch of melting slush and I know that I should put it in the bin or something. It doesn't seem right leaving it in the cold. But I can't do it. I can't bring myself to do anything today.

AFTER JACOB LEFT I decided that I would go home too.

I made up my mind as he disappeared in Hamed's van, leaving me standing on the pavement waving like a fucking idiot. As I climbed the stairwell I had no energy; I didn't want to be here on my own. I thought about phoning Mum first, asking her permission, even though I knew I didn't need to. I still had my key. I could let myself in the back door and she would come rushing downstairs.

'I couldn't do it,' I'd say. 'You were right. I'm too young. I should be at home.'

She would smile and roll her eyes, and we would break into teary laughter.

'Come here, come here.'

She wraps me in her arms. I bury my face in her dressing gown.

'I'm so sorry, Mum.'

'Oh my baby. Baby boy.'

'I tried my best.'

'What will we do with you?'

'Is it too late for me to go to college, do you think?'

She kisses me and I smell her breath, a faint smell of decay. I try to move away, but she's holding too tight.

'You're hurting me a bit.'

'Shhh, shhh.'

'I mean it. Let go.'

'What will we do with you?'

'Stop saying that.' The smell is more powerful, filling the room. It's not her breath. There's something on the kitchen table. I see it over her shoulder. 'What is that? I don't like it, Mummy.'

'Shhh, shut up.'

'I don't like it. You're scaring me.'

'What will we do with you?'

'What's going on?'

The doll is naked, covered in wet mud. Her pale arms stretch across the tabletop, her little face is angled towards us. Button eyes look right through me.

Ha.

It's make believe, that's all.

After Jacob left I imagined going home. But I never did that. I was far too busy going mad.

'You're an asset to the team,' the manager said.

He leant back in his chair and stroked his Rudolf the Red-Nosed Reindeer tie, making the LED in Rudolf's nose flash. I had worked a whole Christmas and was asking for shifts over the New Year too. 'Keep up the hard work, young man, and we'll get you on . . . one of those, uh, National Vocational Qualifications.'

That's how he said it, stretching out each word, like me doing an NVQ would be the making of me.

I can't have given the right response; he let out a slow wheeze and seemed to deflate, 'You're allowed to smile, Matt. I'm paying you a compliment.'

'Can I work the night shift?'

'I've already said you can work the night shift.'

'And the long day?'

He pulled this constipated face at the Duty Rota. 'We'll have to be careful you don't work too many hours. There's legislation about-'

'I need the money.'

He gave me the shifts, he always did. I was working every hour I could to pay my rent, and because I didn't want to be at home by myself. To be honest, I was feeling pretty lonely at this time. So when I wasn't at the old people's home I'd immerse myself in my Special Project.

I never really stopped.

This illness has a work ethic.

Matthew Homes
Flat 607
Terrence House
Kingsdown
Bristol

Wed 10th Feb 2010

Dear Matthew,

Please do get in touch with either myself (07700 900934) or any of the staff at Hope Road (0117 496 0777) as soon as possible. It's important we arrange for you to have your depot injection, which is now a week overdue.

I hope everything is okay,

Denise Lovell
Care Co-ordinator
Brunel CMHT - Bristol

persisent, isn't she?

I'm fine
I'm fine.

fuck off
fuck off
fuck off

148

I'VE GIVEN YOU THE GUIDED TOUR.

You saw it in the corner, and stretching across the far wall. Were you too polite to say anything, to ask any questions? The sprawling tubes and dirt-encrusted jars.

Strange, isn't it?

I didn't know what it was at first because it wasn't me drawing the designs. He was moving my hand, scratching my pen across the sketch pads and the bedroom wall.

His interstellar dust.

His atoms.

I would wake up in my living room, still wearing my work clothes from the night before; a pair of grey trousers and a white nursing tunic, creased and sweaty. My mouth would be dry, my neck and shoulders aching. All around me would be new materials. I couldn't think where they came from. It was the same every day, more stuff appearing. Reaching into my rucksack once I cut my thumb on a shard of glass. The pain sliced through the fog; I had scavenged from wheelie bins and recycling boxes. For a nucleus, an ice-cream tub. Glass jars and bottles for the orbiting electrons. I had filled carrier bags full of damp earth, spilling onto the carpet. There was more plastic tubing stolen from work. Tubes for sucking air from a tank, tubes for pissing into a bag.

And Sellotape. And Blu-tack.

It might even be fun.

As the sharp pain gave way to a dull throbbing, I felt my hands start to move. I could work for hours on end without eating or drinking. Six, seven, eight hours, carefully puncturing holes in jam-smeared lids with the screwdriver from my Swiss Army Knife, feeding in the tubes, and sealing up any gaps.

'Are you home darling?'

I didn't hear her knock. It was only her voice that broke through. The letter box dropped shut.

Nanny Noo was standing in the blue light of the corridor with a Tesco bag in each hand. She smiled, 'I thought I could hear you. I'm not interrupting am I? I was just passing and-'

'You can't come in.'

'I've brought a few groceries, I thought we could-'

'You can't come in, Nanny.'

'But-'

'I'm late for work.'

'It's late, it's dinner time.'

'I'm working the night shift.'

'Then let me drive you. We can quickly put this lot in the kitchen, it'll only take a minute.' She started to push the door to let herself inside. I stayed standing in the way. 'Whatever is the matter?' she asked.

'Nothing.'

'Matthew, sweetheart. You've mud all over your trousers.'

'Do I?'

'Is that blood?'

'What?'

'On your top, there.'

'I cut my thumb.'

'Let me see.'

'I've got to go Nanny, I'm late.'

'You haven't even put a plaster on.' She put down the carrier bags and started to rummage in her handbag. 'I know I've got some somewhere. You never know when-'

'Please don't make a fuss.'

'It's not a fuss. Here we are. Now give me your-'

She reached to take my hand. I pulled away. 'I mean it. I have things to do. You can't just turn up and expect to be let in. I'm busy, I have things to do.'

'Yes. Of course. Of course, sweetheart. I'm sorry.'

I guess she looked a bit hurt. She dropped the

plaster back into her handbag, and fastened the clip.
She started to say something else, but I shut the door.

I watched her through the peephole.

She looked worried, but she didn't knock again. She
lifted her hand to the door and held it there a while,
but she didn't knock. That's the thing with Nanny, she
would never force her company on someone, no matter
how much she might want to.

Ha.

She's like a vampire. She has to be invited in.

I'll tell her that when I next see her. She'll like
that a lot. She visits every other Thursday, but it's
not my turn today. I'll have to remember the vampire
joke for next week. You've got your granddad in you,
she'll laugh. The same wicked sense of humour. She says
she doesn't know what to do with us, but you can tell
she likes it really. What she will NOT like is what
I'm up to now; all this skiving from the Day Centre to
write my story and ignoring the letters from Denise
Lovell and not having my medicine.

She won't like that one bit.

If it wasn't for Nanny Noo I wouldn't give a shit,
but when somebody cares for you as much as she does,
I know it's not nice to make them worry. She'll be
worried this time, and she was worried back then too.
I watched her through the peephole, waiting, hoping.

She left the bags of groceries outside my door, and disappeared.

This is called a genogram.

It's a family tree that doctors draw. It's to help them see which branches bear the rotten fruit.

That's me at the bottom, waving at you. I'm a male, which means I go in a square. And because this is my genogram, I get to go in an extra thick square. Simon is beside me, and he goes in a square too, but with an X through it, which means he's dead.

Up a branch and to the left is my dad.

Hello Dad.

Beside Dad is Uncle Stew, he died of pancreatic cancer when he was thirty-eight years old. So sad, people said. So young, people said. Just goes to show,

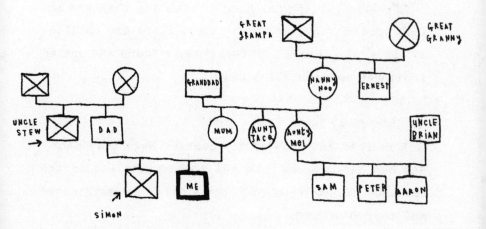

people said. Climbing up again we have Dad's parents;
XX. Dad comes from a long line of dead people.

Mum is a circle, and her side of the tree has a bit
more life to it. That's Aunt Jacqueline beside her, and
then Aunty Mel, who is married - with a horizontal
line - to Uncle Brian. They have three boys; my cousins
Sam, Peter, and Aaron. Keep climbing. Careful now.
Peter fell from a tree once. He hurt himself so badly
that he was in Intensive Care for nearly a week, and
everyone was worried he might die. He didn't though.

No X, see.

Nanny Noo and Granddad are high up. And at the very
top are my Great Granny and Great Grampa, who passed
away within a month of each other when I was still
a baby. Somewhere is a photograph of them holding
me, and Great Grampa is making a funny stinky face
because I have filled my nappy.

If you're getting the hang of climbing then you can
look around and take in the view. There are millions
of trees like this one, but we haven't found the rotten
fruit yet, so don't climb down.

'Is that fizzy pop?'

I reached into one of the carrier bags that Nanny
Noo had left for me. She had reached the end of the
corridor, about to go down the stairwell. She stopped
and turned around.

'There are a few bits and bobs,' she said. 'Make sure you eat the vegetables.'

I swigged at the bottle of Coke. I hadn't drunk anything all day.

'I won't interrupt you, sweetheart.'

'Remember when I stayed with you and Granddad? You know, when I was little. When I came to stay for a bit, after, after Simon-'

'Of course I remember. Is something the matter?'

'Granddad took me to his allotment, to get me out from under your feet. Do you remember that?'

Nanny was back at my door, but I still didn't invite her in. 'Matthew, you're all eyes. You look so tired.'

'Granddad helped me lift up the heavy concrete slabs, so that I could look at the ants.'

Nanny smiled, 'He said you liked doing that. That and playing on your computer games.'

'I did like it.'

'Why don't we have a cup of-'

'I liked it because it reminded me of when Simon and me used to do it. At our house, I mean. In our garden. It made me think about how he wanted an ant farm. Did you know that, Nanny?'

'I didn't, my darling. My memory isn't-'

'No. Well Mum said he wasn't allowed. It wasn't a big deal though, and even if he was disappointed, he would have gotten over it in half a second because he never really cared about stuff like that. I mean he never sulked or anything, did he?'

Nanny smiled again, but it was a sad smile. 'No, he didn't. He was a good boy.'

'He was the best,' I snapped.

Nanny looked startled, it wasn't like me to raise my voice at her. I wasn't angry, it wasn't that. If anything I was frightened, the way adrenalin can seize hold of words and start throwing them out louder and faster, and the way they get muddled up.

'He was the best, Nanny. So I decided to make him one. After he- for his birthday. After he- because dead people still have birthdays, don't they?'

Nanny didn't answer, she reached to stroke my hair.

'Except I never did make it, not back then. I was going to, I took an empty marmalade jar into the garden, but then something happened. When I was looking for the ants, when I was digging in the ground. It's hard to explain. I felt close to him, like he was still here. It's happened other times too, but that was the first time, and I've been thinking about it a lot, and about how I never made him the ant farm.'

I held Nanny's hand against my cheek, she was trembling. 'Do you know what we're made of Nanny?'

She didn't know what to say, and started to say something stupid, to try to change the mood, 'Slugs and snails and puppy dogs' t-'

'I'm serious.'

'You look so tired.'

'We're made of these tiny little things called atoms.
I learnt about it in school once, and I've been reading
about them. Sort of teaching myself about it. Like how
the different atoms look, stuff like that.'

'It's a bit beyond Nanny, my angel.'

'It's beyond everyone. That's just it. This is something
only I know. Do you think memories are made of atoms
too?'

'I really wouldn't-'

'Well they are. They've got to be. Everything is. So
you can build them, you know? Stop them being memories,
and make them real again, with the right ingredients,
like the right sort of atoms and everything.'

'Why don't we get some fresh air?'

'I can show you what I've been making, if you want?'

It must have been hard for her, and it wasn't like I
could properly explain either. Explaining my Special
Project was like trying to explain a dream, how they
can make sense right up until they hit reality, when
they suddenly unravel.

'You can help me if you want.'

Nanny didn't answer. She looked a bit unsteady on
her feet, her face had turned pale.

✳

Nanny Noo visits me every other Thursday, and every
other Thursday she visits Ernest. I've never met him,
and I didn't know anything about him until the school
holidays when Aunty Mel and Uncle Brian and the three
boys came to stay with us. I was seven, or maybe eight.

It was brilliant because whilst the grown-ups
talked over glasses of wine and chunks of cheese, us
children were allowed to stay up late, sharing the
sweets that Nanny Noo and Granddad would bring us.
And it was even more brilliant because our cousins
were better at swearing and fighting than we were,
and even though Sam and Peter were the same ages
as us, Simon and I still idolized them. Aaron's the
oldest. It was his idea that we built a den in Simon's
bedroom, crawling inside with torchlight to scoff
sherbet and Iced Gems, whilst he set about trying to
scare us with stories of what happens when you go to
Big School, how if you don't fit in, or if you wear the
wrong trainers, the older boys will flush your head
down the toilet.

'How would you know?' asked Peter. 'You don't even
start 'til next term.'

'Everyone knows,' insisted Aaron.

'Then you'd better be worried yourself. Because it's
you it's going to happen to.'

'Get lost.'

'Yeah,' said Sam, straight on board for a chance

assault of his big brother. 'It's you it's going to happen to.'

'No it won't.'

'It will. It will.'

Aaron punched Sam hard on the arm, 'Shut up. It won't. Because if anyone comes near me, I'll set Uncle Ernest on them. And if you don't shut up, I'll set him on you too.'

The two younger boys went quiet. Simon scooped another wet finger-load of sherbet. 'Who's Uncle Ernest?'

'What? You don't know who Uncle Ernest is?'

We both shook our heads.

Aaron smiled, and Sam whispered excitedly, 'Tell 'em Aaron. Do it like you told us, with the torch.'

Aaron made us switch our torches off. Then he pressed his under his chin so we could only see his face, floating in the darkness – like you do with ghost stories. He made us swear we'd never breathe a word.

'We swear.'

'Cross your heart and hope to die?'

I nodded, gravely.

'Uncle Ernest is Nanny's brother,' he explained. 'But the reason we never see him is because-'

'Do it properly,' Sam squealed. 'Do the bit with the axe.'

'Shut up, dickhead. You'll ruin it.'

'Yeah, shut up,' said Peter. 'Let Aaron tell it.'

Aaron shoved a Black Jack in his mouth and adjusted his torch. 'The reason we never see him, is because he's locked up. In the cold, dark basement of an insane asylum.'

'A what?'

'You two don't know anything, do you?'

'It's like a prison,' Peter offered helpfully. 'Where the psychos get locked up.'

Simon sucked an audible gasp. I couldn't make out his face properly, but I can still picture it in my mind, even now.

That's a fear when someone you love dies, isn't it? Especially if you're only young when it happens, you might worry that over time you'll stop being able to picture them properly. Or that the sound of their voice will merge into other voices, so that you can no longer be sure how it was they sounded.

I don't worry about that.

Simon's voice was all mischief and excitement as he leaned in close and whispered, 'Is Uncle Ernest a psycho?'

'Is he, Aaron? Is he? Tell us.'

Aaron wiped a glob of Simon's spit from his cheek, 'He wasn't, not when he was little. He was normal, like us.'

'Simon's not normal,' Sam mumbled.

Simon didn't hear him though, or if he did he never

let on. And he didn't see me crush Sam's fingers against the floorboards, making him wail.

Aaron switched off his torch, 'Forget it.'

'No tell us. Tell us.'

'Last chance, I mean it.'

I should say that Aaron's story wasn't true. Some of it was, but not the part with the axe. Nanny's brother has never hurt anyone in his life. Whatever Aaron had once discovered, it wasn't this.

He made it up to scare Peter and Sam, and now he had a chance to scare me and Simon too. That doesn't make him a bad person, because he was just a little boy, and I know Nanny Noo felt terrible for what she did, when she came upstairs, and overheard.

'He was normal,' Aaron said. 'Right up until he went to Big School, when the other children bullied him.'

'And flushed his head down the toilet?'

'Exactly,' said Aaron. 'And worse things too.'

'Is that what made him psycho?' I asked.

'No. What made him psycho, was what the bullies did to Nanny.'

I felt Simon take hold of my hand, 'What did they do?'

'If you shut up, I'm telling you. She went to a different school, for girls. But they used to walk home together, her and Uncle Ernest. And because they lived in the countryside back then, they had to walk through these fields, where there's really tall crops and stuff, so it's easy to hide. And one day that's what the bullies were doing, three or four of them, or maybe even more, and their big brothers too. They were all hiding, waiting for Nanny and Uncle Ernest to come by, and when they did, they all jumped out. And they held Uncle Ernest back.'

Aaron paused for effect.

'Tell 'em about the axe,' Sam squealed.

Aaron couldn't say what happened to Nanny Noo, because he didn't understand it himself. In the adult conversation he had long ago overheard, these details were locked away behind unfamiliar words. I've tried to imagine how Aunty Mel talked about it, turning a family tragedy into an anecdote to share with friends, if she had paused for effect too, if the story was interrupted with the arrival of dessert. I think about how the passing of time makes everything seem less real.

Aaron had spied them from his own Watching Stair, sleepiness sinking over him, then came the words he had understood. Words like guilt and shame and nightmares – the kind of nightmares that drag you from sleep, and leave you reaching for something no longer there.

'He refused to leave his room. For a whole year.'

Aaron stretched out the word year, he was a good storyteller. We were all so engrossed, not one of us heard the footsteps climbing the stairs.

'Whenever anyone tried to see him, he would scream and scream until they left him alone. Then at night they would hear him through the door, talking and laughing, like there was someone else there. Until one morning, he appeared at the breakfast table, with his school uniform on, his hair neatly combed, and he quietly ate his breakfast with Great Grampa and Great Granma and Nanny, as if nothing had happened. He said that he'd had a terrible dream, that Nanny was in it, and he was so pleased it wasn't real. He cleared his plates and kissed her on the cheek, saying he would walk her home from school like normal, but he couldn't walk her there, because he had something important to do first. It wasn't until later that morning, when Great Grampa was in the garden, that he noticed the shed door was unlocked, blowing open in the wind. And as he heard the first-'

Aaron stopped; we thought we could hear something. He was scaring himself as much as us. Simon squeezed my hand tighter. Aaron searched for the right words to finish his story.

He was a good storyteller. He works for a bank now, and every Christmas I get a card from him and his fiancée, who I think is called Jenny or Gemma or one of those names. It always says the same thing: How we must catch up, that we should go for a beer if I ever happen to be in London. It's kind of them to say it, to pretend they think I'm that sort of person, living a life where I might just happen to be in London. Anyway, even if I was that person, I still wouldn't remind Aaron of what a good storyteller he used to be, because I reckon this is one childhood memory he'd rather forget.

He looked slowly between us, making us wait. 'As Great Grampa heard the first terrified screams from across the fields, he looked in his shed, and realized that his axe-'

The roof of the den was suddenly torn away; Nanny Noo was standing over us.

'You little- You little-'

You're getting to know Nanny Noo by now, even if you've never met her. You know the sort of person she is, that she's kind and generous and loving and patient, that she doesn't have a bad word to say about anyone.

'You little shit.'

Aaron tried to say he was sorry, but Nanny was already dragging him across the room. He was too shocked to cry as she put him over her knee, and took off her slipper. Moments later Mum and Aunty Mel appeared in the doorway, their mouths wide open.

'You can help me,' I said again. 'I can show you how it works, Nanny. We can finish it together.'

Nanny looked around my living room; her face was pale. I think she needed to sit down, but there wasn't any space. The whole floor, the chairs, the table, every surface was taken over. I had filled hundreds of bottles and jars with earth, connecting groups of them together with plastic tubing. The Hydrogens were already up and running – they're the easiest to build – a single proton and a single electron. I had made ten of these because we are made of ten per cent hydrogen. The Oxygens took more work, two electrons in the first shell, and six in the outer shell. Then I would pair them up, colliding a pair of electrons from each to make the covalent bonds. This often smashed the glass, so most of the ants had escaped. The carpet was crawling with them.

Nanny pressed a tissue to her lips, 'We need to get you some help.'

'What do you mean? I'm fine. You don't get it, Nanny. I'm going to bring him back.'

'Matthew, please.'

'Don't talk to me like that.'

'Like what?'

'Like Mum does, like you all do. Don't tell me what to do.'

'I wasn't-'

'You were. I should never have let you in, this is private. I knew I couldn't trust you. You're just like the others.'

'Please, I'm worried.'

'Go home then. Leave me alone.'

'I can't. Not like this, try and understand.'

'I'm going to be late, I'll be late for work.'

'Matthew, you can't-'

'Stop it. Don't tell me what I can't do. I've got to, okay? You don't understand. I'm not trying to upset you, Nanny. It isn't that. I'm sorry. I shouldn't have let you in.'

Nanny Noo visits me every other Thursday, and every other Thursday she visits Ernest. She talks about him from time to time. He's handsome and has grown more so with age. He always combs his hair and shaves before she visits him, and he helps to tend the small garden at the special hospital where he has lived for most of his life. Some days are not so good, but that's just the way it is with family. That's what Nanny says.

She's not a bit ashamed of him.

'I'm going to work,' I said. 'I've got to go.'

I don't know how long she stayed. Alone in my kitchen, with night pressing at the window. She cleaned as much as she could, scouring at filth until her hands were sore, until she was too exhausted to carry on. Her brother has a disease, an illness with the shape and sound of a snake. It slithers through the branches of our family tree. It must have broken her heart, to know that I was next.

THEN ONE NIGHT SHIFT. At around 3 a.m.

When I hadn't slept, when I hadn't taken my break because we were short-staffed, and because breaks were deducted from pay, so if I didn't take it I'd get an extra £7.40 towards the rent.

I had just helped a new resident into bed after spotting him moving unsteadily through the gloomy corridors, his pyjama bottoms slipping down over bony hips. I wanted to know something about him, something I could say to help him feel at ease, a reassurance about when his wife might visit, or his children. I switched on his bedside light, unlocked the drawer and took out his folder. Attached with Sellotape to the inside front cover was his personal note. It looked different to the others though, the handwriting was different. That was the first thing I noticed. Most of the notes were written by Barbara, this senior care assistant, who would take real pride in making them all neat. But this one wasn't neat at all. The words wobbled across the page, each letter pressed too hard in pencil. I could picture him doing it, his face scrunched up with the effort. It said,

HELLO my Name is Simon Homes. But you can call me your Brother. I'm scared you will forget me. thats what happens to the people here. We are forgotten. I hate it. Do you remember what we used to do in the mornings? We hid Behind the door until dad came in and then we wrestled him to the ground. that was fun. We had Lots of Fun. I didnt think you would ever Forget. I carried you up the cliff at ocean cove, it was hard But I did it and You were Proud of me, I'm Not going to Let you Forget me matthew. I'm Never going to Let you Forget me. You have to come and Play.

Inside my head is a jigsaw made of trillions and trillions and trillions and trillions of atoms. It might take a while. The old man gripped at my uniform tunic, his brittle fingernails snagging on the poppers. He pulled me so close that his stubble scratched against the tip of my nose.

'Is that you, Simon?' I whispered. 'Is that you in there?'

He stared at me with watery eyes. His voice was distant – in that way so many of them sounded, when they no longer owned their words, but were possessed by them.

'I'm Lost, I'm Lost, I'm Lost,' he said.

I tore myself away.

I'm Lost, I'm Lost, I'm Lost.

In the forecourt the other care assistant was smoking a cigarette under the scrutinizing glare of a security light. 'Jesus Christ, Matt,' she said. 'You look like you've seen a ghost.' Her face was floating towards me, changing shape. I pushed straight past. As I ran out of the gates she was shouting at me to come back. That the shift wasn't over, that she couldn't get the residents up by herself.

I'm Lost, I'm Lost, I'm Lost.

A group of lads poured out of a side street, 'What the fuck are you looking at?'

Their faces were hidden beneath hoods and baseball

caps. It wasn't until I got closer that I could properly
see him, see his face in their faces. You have to come
and play now.

'Is that you, Simon?'

'You what? Look at him, he's off his face. What you
talking about you fucking weirdo?'

'Sorry. I thought-'

'Hey mate, you couldn't lend us a fiver could you?'

'What?'

'We'll give it back.'

'Yeah, I've got-'

I'm Lost, I'm Lost, I'm Lost.

I stumbled into a new morning, blurred at its edges.
The streets stirred to life under a cloudy sky. People
were staring at me, pointing, or turning quickly away.
Each of them had him inside; his many, many, many
atoms, and each of them with his face, his beautiful
smiling face.

It wasn't frightening, it wasn't like that.

It was glorious.

Then things took a turn

for the worse.

MY SHOES WERE MISSING, replaced with yellow foam slippers. I think of this, and I am there. Some memories refuse to be locked in time or place. They follow us, opening a peephole with metallic scratch, and watching through curious eyes. I am there. In front of me is a huge metal door, coated in chipped blue paint. There is no handle on this side. It is not meant to be opened from this side. My pockets are empty, and the belt is missing from my trousers. I have no idea where I am. White light flickers from a caged fluorescent tube above my head. The walls are bare, tiled in dirty ceramic squares. In the far corner is a polished steel toilet bowl with no seat or lid. The air smells of bleach. This body isn't my own, it merges into the space around me so that I cannot feel where I end and the rest of the world begins. I step towards the door, lose balance, stagger sideways, fall hard against the metal toilet. A string of red drips from my lips,

taking a perfect white fleck of tooth enamel into the
bowl. It descends slowly, weightless in the dark water.
The peephole closes. Some memories refuse to be locked
in time or place, they are always present. A person
is saying I have done nothing wrong: You have done
nothing wrong, you're in a Police Cell for your own
safety because you're unwell, confused, disorientated,
lost, lost, lost. I am there. I can taste cotton wool and
the person is saying that I've been sedated, that I fell
against the metal toilet. You nearly passed out they
are saying. They are giving me pain killers. They are
saying it could take a while, it will take some time to
arrange a hospital bed. I will be sent to a PSYCHIATRIC
WARD. Is there anyone they can call, someone who might
be worried about me? I push my tongue into the sodden
cotton wool and let my mouth fill up with the irony
taste of blood. I don't need them to call anyone. Not
now. Not now I have my brother back.

Bristol United
Mental Health Partnership BU

Mr Matthew Homes
Flat 607 Terrence House
Kingsdown
Bristol, BS2 8LC

11.2.2010

Re: Community Treatment Order

Dear Mr Matthew Homes,

I am writing to remind you of your responsibilities under the Community Treatment Order (CTO). In consenting to this CTO you agreed to engage with the full therapeutic programme at Hope Road Day Centre, and to adhere to your medication plan.

You are not currently fulfilling these obligations and it is important we meet to discuss this, and decide how best we can support you. Please attend my clinic at Hope Road Day Centre at **10 a.m. on Monday 15th February**. If you are unable to attend this appointment you must telephone beforehand. If you do not attend this appointment or contact beforehand I will issue a request for you to be brought to hospital for a formal assessment.

In accordance with the plan agreed in your CTO a copy of this letter has been forwarded to your nominated contact – Mrs Susan Homes.

Sincerely,

Dr Edward Clement
Consultant Psychiatrist

KNOCK KNOCK KNOCK

Knock knock KNOCK KNOCK. They are outside, standing
at my door, they are peering through the letter box,
they are listening to me type. They know I'm here.

Nanny Noo will have her hand on Mum's arm, and she
will be saying, try not to worry, he'll be okay, he's
writing his stories. Dad will be pacing the concrete
landing, picking up litter, angry, with no idea where
the anger belongs. And Mum will keep knocking and
knocking and KNOCKING with throbbing knuckles, until
I open the door. I will open the door. I always do.

Nanny Noo will move to hug me, but it will be Mum
who I turn to first. I know her desperation.

'Do you want to come in?' I'll ask.

'Yes please.'

'I'm out of teabags.'

'It doesn't matter.'

'I haven't done a shop in a while.'

'It doesn't matter.'

I'll step over the typewriter, over all the letters I've been ignoring. My parents and Nanny will follow. We'll sit in my living room, except Dad will stay standing, straight-backed, looking out of the window, surveying the city.

'We got the letter from Dr Clement,' Mum will say.

'I figured.'

'He said-'

'I know what he said.'

'You can't do this, sweetheart.'

'Can't I?'

'You'll get unwell, they'll put you back on the ward.'

I will look to Nanny Noo, but she won't say anything. She knows better than to pick sides.

'What do you think, Dad?'

He won't turn around. He'll keep staring out of the window. 'You know what I think.'

KNOCKKNOCK Knock Knock

      Knock knock   knock

           Knock Knock

I will let them in. I always do.

And I will go to the Day Centre: to Art Group, to

Talking Group, to Relaxation Group, and I will do as
I'm told.

I will take my medicine.

how best we can support you

It isn't so bad here.

I've been spending time in the relaxation room. It's just a normal room really, but there are a few beanbags scattered about, and a stereo with cassettes of gentle music and meditation. It's as good a place as any, if you've nothing better to do.

Inside my head is a story. I hoped if I told it, it might make more sense to me. It's hard to explain, but if I could only remember everything, if I could write my thoughts on sheets of paper, something to hold with my hands then – I don't know. Nothing probably. Like I say, it's hard to explain.

In the relaxation room I got thinking about trying one of the jigsaw puzzles. There is a drawer stuffed full of them, and a few more stacked on the shelves. I found myself looking at a thousand-piecer. The picture on the box showed a coastline with sloping cliffs above a pebble beach. Dotted along the cliff path are small wooden huts in different colours, and lined along the top are dozens of caravans, like a neat row of white teeth.

It reminded me a lot of Ocean Cove, and if I looked closer,

maybe I could see two young boys running down the path. Or maybe sitting on the beach together, scrunching dry seaweed between their toes and throwing pebbles at a rock to see who could get closest. If I put my face right up close to the box, perhaps I'd hear them laughing together. Or practising new swear words, and promising not to tell Mum. But that was daydreams. There was nobody in the picture. And inside the box were a thousand pieces of nothing, and even some of them would be missing.

'You alright, mate?' I'm not sure how long *Click-Click-Wink* was standing in the doorway, I hadn't noticed him.

'I'm okay thanks Steve.'

I turned away, pushing a cassette of panpipes or whale song into the stereo and turning up the volume. 'I'm going to listen to this.'

'Do you want to talk?'

'No.'

I didn't say that I'd rather be left alone, but I guess it was obvious because he didn't hang about. He didn't go immediately though. He said, 'I've been meaning to give you this.'

It wasn't a big gesture, or a song and dance. He didn't *click*, *click*. He didn't *wink*. He handed me a small yellow Post-it note, and left the room.

I felt the sticky strip against my finger. It took me a moment to work it out.

User name: MattHomes

Password: Writer_In_Residence

I can get so wrapped up in myself I'm blind to the kindness

179

around me. He didn't have to do that. It isn't so bad here. Right now I'm logged onto the computer as a Writer_In_Residence, and I have a story to finish.

clock watching

I was driven from the police station to the hospital without any sirens – a policeman at the wheel and a social worker sitting beside me in the back, holding my section papers on her knees, absently twisting a paper clip. My mouth was still stuffed with cotton wool from when I fell in the police cell, and I could feel the jagged broken edge of my front tooth against the tip of my tongue. My brother's voice crackled over static on the police radio.

I want to talk about the difference between living and existing, and what it was to be kept on an acute psychiatric ward for day after day after day after day after day after day after day after day after day after day after day after **day** after day etc.

Day 13, for example

7 a.m.

Get woken by a knock on my bedroom door, and the call for morning medication round. I have a metallic taste in my mouth, a side effect of the sleeping tablets.

7.01 a.m.

Sleep.

7.20 a.m.

Get woken again by a second knock. This time the door opens and a nursing assistant walks in and pulls the curtains. She stands at the foot of my bed until I get up. She makes a remark about what a lovely day it is. It isn't a lovely day.

7.22 a.m.

Walk down the corridor in my dressing gown. Wait in a queue for medication that I don't want. Avoid eye-contact with the other patients who are doing the same.

7.28 a.m.

Get given tablets, an assortment of colours and shapes in a plastic cup. Ask the dispensing nurse what they are for?

'The yellow one is to help you relax, and those two white ones are to help with some of the troubling thoughts you've been having. And that other white one is to help with the side effects. You know all of this, Matt.'

'I just like to check.'

'Every morning?'

'Yes. Sorry.'

'You can trust us, you know.'

'Can I?'

They watch me to make sure I swallow them. I always swallow them. They always watch.

7.30 a.m.

Breakfast is Weetabix with lots of sugar and a Mars Bar that Mum brought in. The coffee is decaffeinated. The mugs are provided by Drug Reps. They have the brands of the medication we hate, stamped all over them.

7.45 a.m.

Sit in the high-fenced smokers' garden with other patients. Some of them talk. The manics talk. But they talk crap. Most of us don't say anything.

Those who don't have cigarettes blag off those who do, and promise to pay them back when benefits come through.

We smoke for ages. There is nothing else to do. Nothing. Some of the patients have yellow fingers. One of the patients has brown fingers. We all cough too much. There is literally nothing to do.

8.30 a.m.

A nursing assistant pokes his head around the door. He explains that he is my allocated nurse for the shift. He asks if I would like some one-to-one time? He isn't one of the staff who I feel safe talking to, so I say no. He looks relieved.

8.31 a.m.
Go take a piss.

8.34 a.m.
Continue smoking.

9.30 a.m.
Finish last cigarette. Feel a surge of panic. Try some of the breathing exercises the occupational therapist taught me. A manic lady stubs her cigarette out, and starts playing at nurse. She tells me that breathing exercises help her too. She tells me I'll be fine. She asks me if I would like a cup of tea, but then gets distracted and starts talking to someone else about the different kinds of tea she enjoys. She doesn't seem to notice me leave.

9.40 a.m.
Run a bath. Stuck to the tub are somebody's pubic hairs. I have to swill them away first. There is tightness in my chest. My hands are shaking. The panic is getting worse, it's hard to breathe. Forget bath. Leave bathroom.

9.45 a.m.
Knock on the nursing office door. All of the morning shift are in there. They are chatting over cups of tea, sharing some cake that

was left behind by the night staff.

I feel like I'm interrupting.

'I need some PRN,' I say.

PRN is the name given to medication we can have on an as-required basis. All patients know this.

'I need the one that calms me down,' I say.

'Diazepam? You have that with your regular tablets, Matt. You've already had it this morning. It takes a while to work. You can have some more at lunchtime. Why don't you try your breathing exercises?'

'I have.'

'Why don't you try to distract yourself? You could get dressed.'

This is what we do to distract ourselves. Fun stuff. Like getting dressed.

9.50 a.m.
Put on my combat trousers and green T-shirt. Lace up my boots. Curl up in bed. Sleep.

12.20 p.m.
Get woken by a knock at the door. The lunch trolley has arrived. Get up. Take a piss.

12.25 p.m.
Sit in the dining room with other patients and eat hospital food. It isn't bad. Take double helpings of Victoria Sponge.

12.32 p.m.

A nurse steps into the dining room and gives me my diazepam tablet. She doesn't wait to watch me take it. She knows that I want this one.

12.33 p.m.

Get offered three cigarettes in exchange for the diazepam.

12.45 p.m.

Smoke first cigarette.

12.52 p.m.

Smoke second cigarette.

1.15 p.m.

A lady who I have never met before comes out to the smokers' garden and asks if I am Matt?

'Yes.'

'Hi. I'm an agency nurse on this afternoon, and I was hoping we could have a little chat about how things are?'

'I don't know you.'

'We could get to know each other.'

'Will you work here again?'

'I don't know. I hope so.'

'Can you take me for a walk?'

'I'm not sure. I'll need to see if you're written up for escorted leave.'

'I am.'

'I'll need to check. I'll be right back.'

The lady who I have never met before walks away.

1.35 p.m.

Smoke last cigarette.

1.45 p.m.

The lady (who I have now met once) comes back.

'Sorry I took so long. I couldn't find your notes.'

'That's okay.'

'They were right at the back of the filing cabinet.'

'That's okay.'

'You do have escorted leave written up, but the nurse in charge says we're a bit pressed for staff today, because of sickness. It might not be possible for you to have a walk this afternoon. Did you get one this morning?'

'No.'

'Oh. I'm so sorry about that, Mark.'

'It's Matt.'

'Sorry. The nurse in charge says that your mum comes in around 4 o'clock. You'll be able to go for a walk with her. Is that okay?'

'Yes.'

'It's awful when they're so short of staff, isn't it? Oh I am sorry, Mark.'

2 p.m.

In TV lounge. Listen to an argument between two patients about what they want to watch. Think about cutting my throat. Listen to Simon. Think about whether the TV might be linked to Simon. Think about whether Simon can transmit thoughts through the TV. Think about what I would cut myself with. Think about smashing a coffee mug. Listen to Simon. Sit on my hands. Listen to argument between the two patients. Think about Cloth Dolls. Listen to Simon. Think about Atoms. Listen to Simon. Look at a coffee mug on the magazine table. Listen to Simon. Simon is lonely. Think. Think. Think.

4 p.m.

'Hello sweetheart.'

'I want to go home, Mum.'

'Oh baby.'

'Don't call me that!'

Look through the stuff she's brought. Mars Bars, Golden Virginia, cartons of Ribena and Kia-Ora, a new sketch pad and pens and a camouflage jacket from the army surplus store on Southdown Road. Say thank you, and try to smile.

'Matthew, sweetheart, look at your tooth. Let the nurses take you to a dentist. Please, for me. Or let me take you. The doctor said—'

'It doesn't hurt. Don't make a fuss.'

'I want my handsome smile back.'

'It's not your smile.'

4.10 p.m.

Go for walk around hospital grounds. Tell Mum that I am better. Tell her there is nothing wrong. Ask her if dead people can transmit thoughts through a TV? Try to accept her reassurances. Try to remember she is on my side. Tell her that I am better. Ask her if I am better?

5.30 p.m.

Mum leaves. Dinner arrives. Eat.

5.50 p.m.

Sit in the smokers' garden with other patients. Some of them talk. The manics talk. But they talk crap. Most of us don't say anything. Those who don't have cigarettes blag off of me, and promise they'll pay me back when their benefits come through. There is nothing to do.

6.30 p.m.

Take a shit, then go to bedroom and try to masturbate. Fail.

6.45 p.m.

Back in smokers' garden. It's getting cold.

7.05 p.m.

Pace up and down the corridor. There is another pacer – a black man with long greying dreadlocks and an open shirt showing his chest. We keep passing each other in the middle. We smile at each other. This is fun. Up and down the corridor, smiling each time we pass. Saying hello and goodbye. We start to pace quicker so that we reach each other sooner. We start to run. We laugh each time we meet, doing clumsy High-Fives. A nurse comes out of the office and asks us to settle down.

7.18 p.m.

Back in smokers' garden. It isn't really a garden, it's a claustrophobic square with a few chairs, and dead butt ends littering concrete slabs. There is literally nothing to do.

7.45 p.m.

Go to make a cup of tea in the kitchen. Two patients are snogging. They ask me what I'm looking at? I leave before the kettle boils.

7.47 p.m.

Back in smokers' garden. Nothing.

9.40 p.m.

It's dark, night-time, there is mud in my mouth, in my eyes, and the rain keeps falling. I am trying to carry him, but the ground is wet. I lift him and fall, lift him and fall, and he is silent. His arms hang lifeless at his sides. I am begging him to say something, Please! Say something! I fall again, and I am holding him, holding his face to mine, holding him so close I can feel his warmth leave, and I am begging him to say something. Please. Please. Talk to me.

10 p.m.

Called for evening meds. Wait in a queue for medication that I don't want. Avoid eye-contact with the other patients who are doing the same.

10.08 p.m.

Get given tablets, an assortment of colours and shapes in a plastic cup. Ask what they are for?

'They're your tablets, Matt. You need to take them.'

'The other nurses tell me what they're for.'

'Then you know.'

'Please tell me.'

'Okay. These two are to help with the difficult thoughts, and the voices.'

'I don't hear voices.'*

'Well—'

'I don't hear voices, okay? It's my brother, for fuck's sake! How many times do I need to tell you people this?'

'Please don't swear at me, Matt. I find it intimidating.'

'I'm not trying to intimidate you!'

'Okay, well please don't shout then.'

'I didn't mean to intimidate you. I didn't mean that.'

'Shall I tell you what the other tablets are for?'

'Yes please.'

'This one is because you've been having some side effects, it should help with the dribbling at night. And this one is your sleeping tablet. Actually, you can try without this if you want?'

'Which one?'

'The sleeper. It's PRN. You don't have to have it.'

'I'll try without. It leaves a taste in my mouth.'

'A metal taste?'

'Yes.'

'That's very common. See how you get on without it.'

'I didn't mean to intimidate you, I'm sorry.'

10.30 p.m.

Go to bed. Wait for sleep.

10.36 p.m.

There is a knock at my door, someone says I have a phone call.

The night-shift nurse is reading a magazine at reception. She watches me lift the receiver.

'Hello.'

'Sorry I didn't make it today.'

'That's okay.'

'It's my ma, she's—'

'It's okay.'

'How are you, anyway?'

'It's Jacob, right?'

'Yeah man, you know it is.'

The nurse pretends to read her magazine. Pressing the phone tightly to my cheek, I whisper. 'Thank you for calling.'

There is silence at the other end. Then, 'I can't hear you, Matt.'

'How's your mum?' I ask.

'She's alright. She got a new chair today. She's bitching about it – says the head rest makes her look disabled. I mean, for fuck's sake. How disabled does she need to be?'

Someone laughs. There's someone with him. I ask what he's up to?

'How are you, anyway?' he asks.

'What you up to?' I ask again.

'Having a smoke with Hamed.'

'Yeah?'

'Yeah, man. He's got some killer Green. I'll bring you some in next time if you want? I would have come today, but you know how it is with—'

'Don't worry about it.'

I don't want him to be smoking with Hamed. I don't know Hamed. I don't want the world to keep turning without me on it.

'How are you, anyway?' he asks.

'Ask your fucking brother.'

'I can't hear you?'

'I'm locked up.'

There is silence. Then, 'What did you say?'

'I said I'm locked up.'

'No, before that. You said something about my brother?'

I don't answer. The nurse flips a page of her magazine, staring straight at me.

'Come in tomorrow, if you want.'

'I don't know about tomorrow, mate. It's just—'

'Or the next day.' I'm clenching the receiver so tight my

knuckles ache. I can hear the start-up tune of his XBox 360.

'Mate, I've gotta go. It's my ma. She's calling me. I'll give you a shout soon, yeah. Catch you later.'

10.39 p.m.
Listen to the automated telephone voice – The other person has cleared the line. The other person has cleared the line. The other person has enough shit to worry about without you to deal with too.

10.41 p.m.
Hang up.

10.45 p.m.
Lie in bed. Twisting my sheets into knots.

12.30 a.m.
Get up and request sleeping tablets. One more cigarette. Climb into bed. Wait for sleep.

1 a.m.
The viewing slat on my door lifts. Torchlight shines against my chest for a single rise and fall. The viewing slat drops.

2 a.m.
As above.

3 a.m.
As above.

7 a.m.
Get woken by a knock on my bedroom door, and the call for morning medication round. I have a metallic taste in my mouth, a side effect of the sleeping tablets.

(Repeat)

*I don't hear voices

In the smokers' garden dry leaves scurried across the concrete slabs, or trembled at the high wire fence.

I would watch them, waiting for him to reveal himself. If I kept my mind sharp, stayed alert, he would speak. He had chosen to be with me, not Mum or Dad or his friends from school. He didn't talk to the doctors, the nurses; I couldn't expect them to understand.

In my room, at night, if I stayed awake, filling the sink with cold water to splash my face, if the tap choked and spluttered before the water came, he was saying, I'm lonely. When I opened a bottle of Dr Pepper and the caramel bubbles fizzed over the rim, he was asking me to come and play. He could speak through an itch, the certainty of a sneeze, the after-taste of tablets, or the way sugar fell from a spoon.

He was everywhere, and in everything. The smallest parts of him; electrons, protons, neutrons.

If I were more perceptive, if my senses weren't so blunted by the medicine, I'd be better able to decipher, understand what he meant by the movement of the leaves, or the sideways glances of patients as we sucked endlessly at cigarettes.

drawing behaviour

Drawing was a way to be somewhere else.

Mum brought me a new sketch pad onto the ward, and the right type of pencils and ink pens. So when I wasn't smoking or trying to sleep, I did sketches from my imagination.

I'm an okay artist. Mum thinks I'm better than I am. At home she has a drawer full of my pictures and stories, dating way back from when I was little.

For her fiftieth birthday I wanted to give her something special. I was fifteen and knew I wasn't the easiest teenager to live with. I wanted to let her know that I loved her, and I still cared. I'd decided to try a portrait of her, but when I ran it past Dad he said, 'Don't you think she'd prefer one of the family?' I knew he was right, so I set about doing that instead. I decided to draw us on the couch together, but I wanted it to be a surprise, so what I did was come into the living room whenever she was watching TV or reading or whatever, and I'd make secret notes and partial sketches to help me remember details, like the way she holds her neck slightly to the side, and how she crosses her legs, with one foot wrapped right behind the other ankle.

I think personalities are hidden in these details, and if you capture them properly, you capture the person.

This was a long time after Simon died, and it wasn't like we thought about him every day. Or I guess Mum might have, but I didn't. Not so much. And nowhere near as much as I do now. But I decided it wasn't right to have a family portrait without him in it.

In the end I did something I'm really proud of, and I don't get to say that often. I took one of the framed pictures of Simon from the mantelpiece – the one of him beaming proudly in his new school uniform – and drew it on the little table beside the couch, where we kept the newspapers. I drew Mum beside him, then myself between her and Dad. I got Mum's crossed legs pretty much perfect, and I did Dad biting at his bottom lip like he does when he concentrates. Self-portraits are the hardest. It's hard to capture your own self, or even know what it is. In the end I decided to do myself with a sketchbook on my knees, drawing a picture. And if you look carefully, you can make out the top of the picture – and it's the one we're in.

I think that's sort of what I'm doing now too. I am writing myself into my own story, and I am telling it from within.

On the ward, I sat in the smokers' garden, and pictured my flat. I thought about my kitchen and drew it, complete with chipped tiles and blistered wallpaper. Nanny Noo is standing at the sink peeling vegetables, with her packet of menthol cigarettes on the counter. When I draw pictures from my mind, I like to think about where I would be standing if I were actually there. I'm standing in the hall, just out of sight. I even put a bit of the door frame along one side. It wasn't bad, and I was really concentrating on it, so I didn't notice the other patient glancing over.

Her name was Jessica, I think. She said she liked my picture, and would I maybe draw her too?

When you are drawing something that is in front of you – rather than from the place in your mind where pictures form – it makes you think more about where you are, and feel yourself actually being there. I don't know if that makes much sense, but it's true.

Jessica once had a baby girl named Lilly, but Lilly was evil. This is what Jessica told me to explain the scars. She invited me into her room and closed the curtains. I said it would help to draw her in natural light, but then she unbuttoned her blouse and took off her bra and we sat in silence for a while.

I could have drawn other patients; perhaps Tammy in her pink dressing gown, holding her teddy. She would cry at how beautiful it was to be seen. I could have sketched the man who checked his shoes every ten minutes for listening devices, or captured the blur and chaos of Euan as he bounced off the walls, seeking excitement. I could have drawn Susan, who would spend lunchtimes gathering the salt shakers from every table until Alex screamed at her to stop it and they both descended into hour-long sulks. There was Shreena's hair, matted and greasy, that she would pull out in clumps and leave on surfaces – I could have drawn those, perhaps catching her personality in the parts she chose to shed.

There were nineteen beds on the ward, with new patients

arriving as others checked out – like the world's wackiest hotel. I could have drawn them all. But I only drew Jessica. I drew her half naked in the half-light of her room. And I drew her scars. She'd fed the devil at her breasts, then cut the pain away.

'It's perfect, Matt. Thank you.'

'Okay.'

'It's really perfect.'

'You're welcome.'

I didn't want to think about where I was, to feel myself being there. I didn't draw any other patients, and I didn't draw the charge nurse in her office the next day, holding my sketch of Jessica, and slowly shaking her head.

'She said it was perfect,' I protested weakly.

'It's not the point, Matthew.'

'She asked me to do it.'

'She felt pressured. And she isn't well.'

'This is fucking bollocks.'

'Please don't use that language.'

'Well it is. It is fucking bollocks. I didn't even want to draw the bitch.'

'Matthew, that's enough. Nobody is telling you off. This is about boundaries. Everyone is here to get better, and that includes you. I'm asking that you don't go in other patients' rooms, even if they do invite you.'

'She did.'

'And I'm asking you not to draw the people here. Between you and me, I see you're talented.'

'Please don't.'

'Well—'

'Don't. I don't need this. I won't draw anyone else. I'd decided that already. I never wanted to in the first place.'

'Okay. Well, let's leave it at that then. And Matt, I wasn't telling you off.'

'Can I go?'

'Of course.'

I drew Nanny Noo in my kitchen, and the bench at the park where I used to sit with Jacob when we bunked off school. I drew the outside world. If you ever visit my parents' house, you'll see my family portrait above the fireplace. Mum loved it. Drawing is a way to be somewhere else.

writing behaviour

Thomas half ran, half stumbled – wearing his tomato ketchup-stained tracksuit bottoms, and his Bristol City football shirt.

The alarm made a startled, violent sound.

He made it down the slope to where the water feature wasn't working, before being caught by Nurse This and Nurse That, and a Third Nurse who was just that moment arriving to work and still had his luminous yellow bicycle clip on around his ankle. I opened my bedroom window as far as it would go, which wasn't very far – obviously. It was impossible to hear what Nurse This was saying over the shouting.

Thomas wasn't shouting at her. He was shouting at God, thrusting a Gideon's Bible towards heaven, howling FuckYoooou, FuckYoooou, FuckYoooou.

He was the closest I got to having a friend in that place. We didn't talk much, but since the evening we paced the corridor together giving High-Fives, he always ate beside me at lunch, and I shared my tobacco whenever he ran out. The two things he did sometimes talk about were God, and Bristol City Football

Club. These were his two great loves, though looking at him now, I guess he'd fallen out with one of them.

Nurse This placed a hand on his back, beneath his long greying dreadlocks. I couldn't hear her from my room, but she might have said, 'It's okay, Thomas. It's going to be okay. Please. Come back on the ward.'

It would have been kinder to have locked the front door in the first place – except they preferred not to if the ward was calm, so that the voluntary patients wouldn't feel caged. But it wouldn't be left unlocked after this. No time soon anyway. Thomas was giving a hearty FuckYoooou to any chance of that.

More nurses gathered around him, sharing glances, moving into position.

I decided to say a prayer, asking God to show a bit of mercy or whatever. I don't know much about praying, so I rummaged about for my copy of the Gideon's Bible. There was one in every room. I figured it might give me some pointers.

I found it in my bedside drawer, under my Nintendo DS, and a patient information leaflet about the Mental Health Act.

It was too late. They move so quickly. If I remember right, it was Nurse Whoever gripping hold of Thomas's head. He was black like Thomas, but with the kind of brick shit-house build you only get by putting in serious hours at the gym. And he had these wonky yellow teeth that looked like they were trying to escape his mouth whenever he smiled.

Nobody was smiling now.

Nurse That had grabbed an arm, holding on so tightly that his knuckles were turning white. He was this gaunt-looking guy with flesh nearly as pale as mine, and this permanently sympathetic look on his face – with his head forever cocked over to the side. He was usually all *Hmm, and how did that make you feel?* But evidently he had a decent grip on him too. Thomas was struggling, but getting nowhere.

Nurse Just Thought I'd Join In For The Hell Of It was on the other arm. He was middle-aged, bald, fat, and sweaty.

I'm being unkind, aren't I?

It's not like me to be nasty about how people look. I don't give a shit about that sort of thing. I'm just feeling pissed off at the moment. I feel angry sometimes when I think about the things I saw in hospital. I feel pissed off now, and I felt pissed off at the time, watching Thomas struggle so hard to escape that his beloved Bristol City shirt caught against the handrail, tearing a huge rip into it.

'It's going to be okay, Thomas. It's going to be okay,' Nurse This was saying.

As they dragged him back up the slope, I put my Bible away. Half a pouch of Golden Virginia later, the lunch trolley arrived, and what passed for normality in that place continued.

Thomas didn't come to eat. So I went to the kitchen, made two cups of tea, each with three sugars, and when I was certain nobody was watching, I walked down the corridor and tapped on his door.

'Thomas, are you in there?'

He didn't answer.

'I brought you a cup of tea, mate.'

I lifted the viewing slat a few centimetres. He was curled up on his bed, on his side, with a pillow pressed between his legs, with his eyes closed, sucking his thumb. His torn shirt was draped across the chair, with his Bible placed on top.

I'd never seen a grown man sleeping like that. He looked peaceful, I thought. He looked faraway. Partially visible above the waistband of his tracksuit bottoms, were two small round sticking plasters.

I'd not been sleeping well myself.

I felt envious.

That afternoon I asked if someone could take me to my flat. I hadn't been home in weeks and I needed to check my post. That's what I told them, anyway.

The nurse with the bicycle clip unlocked the main door. I held it open for Nurse This, because Nanny Noo calls me a gentleman.

'Honestly, Matt. This taxi company. They call the office to say they're waiting, you come out, they're nowhere to be seen. Every single bloody time.'

If you know Bristol, you probably know Southdown Hospital. It isn't an asylum or mad house, or whatever you call them. It's a regular hospital, but it has a psychiatric unit too. Before I went there I never knew such places even existed. We walked through the tunnel, separating Crazy Crazy NutsNuts Ward from the general wards, and were alongside the maternity wing, where taxis stop.

It was cold and the sky was grey and overcast. It felt nice to be outside though. Nurse This pulled her scarf above her chin.

She shivered. 'Sorry. I don't know why I'm venting at you. It's certainly not your fault.'

'It looked like a difficult morning,' I offered.

'Why do you say that?'

'Well— I don't know, the thing with Thomas.'

She shook her head, 'I'm so sorry you saw that. It can't be nice to see something like—'

'Is he okay?'

'He's fine, Matt.'

A man hurried past, clutching a bunch of flowers, a huge teddy bear gripped under his arm.

'Did you sedate him? Is that what it's called?'

'Um— I can't talk about other patients. I don't mean to be rude, but I wouldn't talk about you either.'

There was nothing else to say, but the silence felt too heavy. Too uncomfortable to hold. So I tried, 'I was born here. Is that the building where babies are born?'

'Mm-hmm.'

'Then I was born in there. That was the last time I've been in hospital, before now.'

'Really. No broken bones?'

'Nope.'

I could have told her about the countless hours spent at hospitals with Simon, about our Saturday trips to Old Lane Hospital, waiting in the car with Dad, sitting beside him in the front, playing I spy, whilst Mum took Simon in for his Speech Therapy.

Eventually I'd spy them coming back out, skipping across the car park with Simon practising his vowel sounds. Dad would pretend not to notice them coming, and I'd say, 'I spy with my little eye something beginning with *M* and *S*.'

He'd make deliberately stupid guesses like, 'Hmm, Marks & Spencer?' Or, 'Let me think. Mouldy Spuds?' It wasn't even funny, but he made it funny, or else I just wanted it to be. I would howl with laughter.

I could have told Nurse This about that, but a taxi pulled up and she said, 'Here we go, let's get your post.'

I buckled my seatbelt, still holding a memory of Mum turfing me into the back with Simon, kissing Dad on the cheek, asking, 'Will you ever let us in on the joke?'

Saturdays after Speech Therapy was when we went to see Grandma. Dad's mum. She was older than Nanny Noo. She died a long time ago. I think I told you that.

X.

I can't picture her face.

There was a room at the back of her house, which she called the library. It was too small to place a chair, and there were no windows. The door and a tall free-standing lamp took up the space on one side, but the other three walls had shelves lined with hundreds and hundreds of books. I didn't go in often because it was claustrophobic, and a bit scary. It was cold and gloomy, and too far from the reassuring warmth of adult voices in the lounge. I did go in once though, when Simon was annoying me with his vowels, and I wanted to be by myself. I remember running my fingers across the books, reading the authors' names with the lamp light and playing a game in my head. I decided each name on each spine was the person who the book had been written for, rather than who had written it. I decided everyone in the world had a book with their name on, and if I searched hard enough I'd eventually find mine.

I can't have believed it was true, but later, eating cakes and malt loaf at the kitchen table, I told the grown-ups as though I did believe it, like it was my firmest conviction.

Grandma said, 'Isn't he lovely?'

Dad said, 'If you want a book with your name, sunshine, you'll have to write it yourself.'

Nurse This stood at my door like a security guard as I rifled through all the credit card offers and Domino's Pizza flyers piled up on the mat. There was no important mail for me. I wasn't expecting any. I hadn't really come home to pick up the post.

I walked through the coolness of the hall, past the kitchen. Cleaned-out bottles from my Special Project were standing, upturned on the draining board. There was still more of it in the living room, but it had been pushed up neatly against the back wall. Nothing had been thrown away though. That was the deal.

The carpet had been cleaned, and there was a faint smell of fresh paint lingering in the air.

From my small wooden table I picked up one of my A4 ruled notepads. I flipped through it and tore out the pages I'd already scribbled on. I didn't want to see them. I couldn't let myself get sucked back in. About a quarter of it was blank, and that would have to do. Mum had brought me good drawing paper to the

ward, but I didn't want to waste that for writing on. I figured I
might start taking some notes. Just a few observations – what
the nurses looked like, if they had wonky yellow teeth trying to
escape their mouths, that sort of thing. Just in case I ever wanted
to write about it all properly. You have to be careful taking notes
in a mental hospital though, that's what The Pig says. It was him
who would teach me about Writing Behaviour, but I didn't know
him yet.

The notepad wasn't why I'd come either.

What I'd come for was in my bedroom. I hoped it was, anyway.
The paint smell was more powerful in here. I don't like to think
about how my dad must have felt. Alone in my room, quietly painting over the madness that I'd covered the walls with. Mum would
have offered to help, of course – to come with him. But he would
have played it down. He would have said it wasn't so bad. Just a
quick lick here and there is all that was needed, she should go
and see her parents. He'd manage fine on his own.

Hardly any daylight made it through the small window. I
flicked the light on. It was then that I saw he'd written something
himself. I can't say this for certain, but I'd bet any money this was
the first and only time that my dad has ever graffitied on a wall.
You probably don't know him, but you will know people like him.
Everyone knows people who would graffiti on walls, and people
who would never. Not even in a toilet cubicle or a phone box.
I like that my dad is someone who wouldn't.

But beside the light switch, he had written something. I was
never meant to read it. I know this because he would paint over

it when he came back to do the second coat. And he had no way of knowing that I'd be brought home on this one day to collect my post. I ran my fingers across the words, written lightly in ball-point pen. What he'd written was:

We'll beat this thing mon ami. We'll beat this thing together.

I was fairly dosed up on the pills to relax me, but still a tightness gripped at my chest. It was the thought of his sadness. It was the fear that he was wrong.

As fast as I could, I rummaged through my drawers. I needed to get out of there.

'Is everything okay?' Nurse This asked.

I practically knocked her over, I came out so fast. 'I want to go. Sorry. Can we go now?'

She looked at my single carrier bag, clutched to my chest. 'Is that all you're collecting?'

'Yeah. Thanks for bringing me. Can we go?'

'Of course. But might it be an idea to—'

'Please. This is all I want.'

'Okay. The taxi's still waiting. We can go right now.'

'Sorry. Thank you. Thank you.'

Thomas didn't answer when I tapped on his door again. He was still sound asleep.

I walked in as quietly as I could, but I don't think I would have woken him up if I'd gone in with drums.

THE SHOCK OF THE FALL

I took out the shirt from my carrier bag. I don't even like foot-ball. God knows how I ended up with a Bristol City shirt. It had been scrunched up in with my other T-shirts for as long as I can remember. Perhaps waiting for this very moment. It must have been a hundred seasons out of date, but it was a hundred seasons out of date without a huge rip through it.

I carefully draped it over him, 'There you go, mate.'

He didn't even stir.

empty dull thud

Only fifteen minutes today, then puncture time. I have a few compliance problems with tablets, the answer – a long, sharp needle.

Every other week, alternate sides.

I'd rather not think about it now. It's best not to think until the injection is actually going in.

Repetitive, aren't I?

I live a Cut & Paste kind of life.

There's a strange atmosphere here today. It's hard to explain. You could cut it with a knife, that's what Nanny Noo would say. The staff keep disappearing into the back office, where it's all whispers and grave looks. It's not like we can't see them; there's a fucking window. Then they're out here being extra bright and breezy with us, like everything is tickety-boo. Except they look like shit. I don't mean that to sound nasty. I mean they look tired is all. Or stressed. I feel a bit sorry for them if anything. Right now Jeanette, who runs Art Group, is talking to Patricia in her whispery enthusiastic way, but you can tell that it's sort of put on, like she's just going through the motions.

Maybe I'm reading too much into it all. I was up too late last night, drinking with The Pig. We've had a couple this morning too. The Pig isn't a name, The Pig is a label.

That's what I've been thinking about.

It's a label he's given himself, to slap over the labels that other people give him. He's stuck it over HOMELESS and PISS ARTIST, to cover them up. He's dead clever. He slurs a bit and gets distracted, but if you take the time to listen, he's one of those people with a million facts lodged in his head. It was The Pig who taught me about Writing Behaviour. He first mentioned it one time we were drunk together, when I let my guard down, rambling on about the hassle I get from Denise and *Click-Click-Wink* and Dr Clement and the other big shots who get paid to control my life.

Now he talks about it a lot. He gets fairly repetitive when he's been drinking, and he drinks fairly repetitively. I guess he lives a Cut & Paste life too.

He took a swig of Special Brew, 'It was back in the seventies, Lad. Before you were born. But don't let that fool you. Nothing changes.'

Here's what happened

In the 1970s, a group of researchers got themselves deliberately confined to mental asylums across the United States. They did this by pretending to hear voices. They pretended to hear a voice saying, Empty, Dull and Thud.

But as soon as they were admitted to the wards, they stopped pretending, and never mentioned the voice again.

And here's the mad part

The hospital staff outright refused to believe they were better, and kept them locked up anyway – some of them for months on end – each forced into accepting they had a mental illness, and agreeing to take drugs as a condition of their release. This is what labels do. They stick.

If people think you're MAD, then everything you do, everything you think, will have MAD stamped across it.

One of the researchers kept a notebook – he wrote about how he was holding up, what the food was like, that sort of thing. When the experiment was over, he got to read his other notes, the notes his doctors and nurses had been making. They'd observed him scribbling away in his notebook, and recorded it as: Patient is engaging in writing behaviour.

What does that even mean?

I'm not playing dumb. I honestly don't have a clue what that means. Is it what I'm doing? Am I engaging in writing behaviour? I draw pictures too. Is that drawing behaviour? Between you and me, I might take a shit in a bit. Is that engaging in shitting behaviour?

All I know is what The Pig says. We say it together, like a

mantra, like a special handshake. We open a fresh can, and as it froths over our fingers, The Pig snorts, 'You might not beat the wankers, Lad.'

Then we tap our cans together and shout as loud as we can, at the night, at passing traffic. 'But you can't stop fighting!'

I know it's stupid, but it kind of helps.

Anyway, I have to go.

Denise has just appeared at the end of the corridor, 'Whenever you're ready, Matt.'

I'd usually keep her waiting. Keep on fighting. But she looks stressed out, and to be honest, I can't help but feel a bit sorry for her. I'm serious, you could cut it with a knife here today. You could cut it with the crappy blunt scissors they give us in Art Group. Something definitely isn't right.

open wide

We watched EastEnders on the big green couch.

Mum and Dad and me sitting together, which is how it always was because Simon preferred to sit cross-legged on the carpet – with his face right up close to the television.

This was the episode when Bianca left Walford, but it was a long time ago. I only remember because Simon had a crush on her. It felt poignant, I guess. Or just sad. Impossibly sad. This was our new family portrait – the three of us, staring at the space where Simon should have been.

I already told you this.

I said how EastEnders was a ritual, that we videoed it if we weren't going to be in. I didn't mention it again though, because the episode when Bianca left was the end of the ritual. It was the last time we watched EastEnders as a family, and it was the last episode I watched, full stop. Until nearly a decade later. I had finished my tobacco. I had taken my last PRN. There was nothing to do, but sit in the patients' TV lounge, in one of the stained and sunken armchairs, trying to ignore the nausea, headache, hunger, stiffness, and exhaustion caused by two white tablets, twice a day.

The TV lounge was busier than usual. Extra chairs had been brought through from the dining room, and a couple of nurses hovered at the door. This was an episode everyone wanted to watch.

He was in the theme tune, somewhere. He was in the map of London, as the camera twists and lifts away.

Sometimes the whole world can feel like the small print you find at the bottom of adverts, so everyday stuff like a smile or handshake becomes loaded with conflicting messages. This wasn't a smile or handshake, but an episode of EastEnders. It was the episode where after nearly ten years' absence, Bianca finally returned. She had red hair and freckles.

I could have told myself it was a coincidence, these things happen. People are forever telling me to look for evidence, to think about what is likely and what is unlikely. I could have made my hands into fists, pushed knuckles hard against my temples, and searched my thoughts for a rational explanation.

It would have been hopeless though, because even now, I can't quite believe he wasn't trying to tell me something.

That night I couldn't settle.

I must have walked the corridor a hundred times, my bare feet getting cold on the floor. Each time I'd see the nursing assistant with his bunch of keys and his tattered red clipboard. Sometimes he'd be sitting in the bright white light at the front desk,

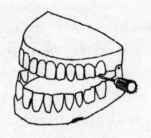

other times he'd be lurking in the shadows, peering through the viewing slats into patient bedrooms. Occasionally he'd raise an eyebrow in my direction, and scan his list for my name.

The staff took turns on observation duty – checking the whole ward every fifteen minutes to make sure nobody had done a runner, or worse. I know this because I observed. They observed me. And I observed them.

When your big brother is calling, when it's finally time to go and play, if you need to escape from a psychiatric ward – the first thing to do is observe.

The next morning I stood sweating into my dressing gown, whilst the nurse selected my tablets from the trolley, popping them through foil and dropping them into a little plastic pot.

'Here you go, Matt.'

'Will you tell me what they're for?'

'Why don't you tell me?'

'I can't remember.'

'I think you can, if you try.'

I was getting to know this nurse quite well. Her name was Claire, or maybe Anna.

'Have a go,' she said. 'They're your tablets, not mine.'

'Did you watch EastEnders?'

'Sudden change of subject—'

'Did you?'

'When?'

'Yesterday. Did you?'

'I don't follow it. Was it good?'

'I'm not sure.'

She handed me the pot of tablets, and filled a second pot with water from a jug.

On psychiatric wards the nurses don't look like nurses. They don't wear uniforms like we did at the care home, and they don't run around carrying straitjackets like you see in films. Claire-or-maybe-Anna wore a pair of jeans and a cardigan. She had a lip-ring, and streaks of purple in her hair. She can't have been more than a few years older than me.

'It's important you talk,' she said at last. 'If you don't open up, say how you're feeling, how can anyone know how to help?'

That's the kind of thing they were always saying. Mostly I wouldn't respond, but this time I did. 'My tooth hurts,' I said. 'Where I chipped it. Mum keeps going on at me. She says she wants my smile back. If you're not too busy—'

'You want to go to the dentist?'

'Only if you're not too busy.'

It wasn't like me to ask for anything, and she was clearly pleased that I had. These are the moments they call progress; something to write up in their notes. I know this because I observed. They observed me. And I observed them.

'Of course we can go. Absolutely we can. Are you registered with a dentist?'

I shook my head and turned away – not wanting to lie out loud, not wanting her to see my thoughts.

'Not to worry,' she said. 'There's the Emergency Clinic by the train station. We can sometimes get a slot there. Do you know what, Matt? The policeman who brought you here felt so bad you hurt yourself on his watch, he wanted to take you to the dentist himself.'

'Why didn't he then?'

I sort of asked that in an angry way. I didn't mean to, but that's the way it came out. I'm no good at long conversations. I could feel myself sweating, feel it soaking into the back of my dressing gown.

Perhaps Claire-or-maybe-Anna was sweating too. 'Well, they're not— It doesn't— It doesn't work that way because of you being on a section. And you were so confused, it was important you came here first. But he was seeking assurances we'd go as soon as we could. And, well, look, why don't you get dressed, and I'll see what I can arrange as soon as I've finished up here?'

I stood at the sink, watching myself in the mirror.

I hooked a finger behind my tongue and scooped out the chalky mush of tablets, making myself gag. Then I swilled the evidence down the plughole.

It was turning into a bright morning. The curtains in my room were really thin and didn't properly reach down to the window ledge. I kept an ashtray on the ledge. We weren't supposed to smoke in our rooms, but I'd started to anyway, and they weren't being too strict about it. I'd borrowed the ashtray from another patient, in exchange for a few cartons of Kia-Ora. It was one of those heavy cut-glass ones that you used to see in pubs, and the way the morning sunlight hit it, chunks of rainbow were cast across my bedding.

I took off my dressing gown and lay naked on my bed, letting the rainbows fall across my skin. My restless night was catching up with me. I was drifting into the colours, thinking how beautiful they were, when I heard a sort of growling noise.

'Hello, who's there?' The noise growled again. It was coming from under my bed. 'Who is that? Stop it. Answer me.'

Then it broke into a giggle, and I knew exactly who it was. I didn't get out of bed, I just leant over the side and slowly lifted the overhanging sheets. The giggle turned to a squeal of delight.

'I knew it was you.'

His face was painted orange with black stripes, and the tip of his nose was a smudge of black with lines drawn for whiskers.

'I'm a tiger,' he grinned. 'Do I look like a tiger?'

'The best one ever,' I smiled.

He growled again. Then he wriggled out on his belly across the floor, 'I look like a tiger, but I'm slithering like a snake.'

He always struggled with the letter S, a lot of his time in Speech Therapy was spent on that. He'd got slithering like a snake pretty good though, and I knew he'd want to hear it.

'Very good,' I said. 'You're getting really good, Simon.'

He beamed with pride, then pounced, throwing his arms around me. I let myself fall under his weight. It felt so good to hold him, I could hardly breathe.

His face scrunched up, 'What were you doing at the sink, Matthew?'

'Were you spying on me?'

He nodded, making his nods deliberately too big, bending from the waist, laughing, 'I saw you! I saw you!'

'Then you know what I was doing.'

He was over at the sink now, peering down the plughole. He could move anywhere in a blink, he could hurtle through time. 'Why did you spit out your medicine? Won't you get sick?'

'You want us to play together, don't you?'

He looked at me, his expression the most serious I had ever seen. 'Forever,' he said. 'I want you to play with me forever.'

It frightened me a bit, how serious he looked. I felt a shiver of cold and pulled the blanket around myself.

'I'm eight,' he said out of nowhere. He counted out eight fingers in the air. Then with deep concentration, his tongue sticking out, he lowered two of them. 'So you're six!'

'No. I'm not six any more.'

He stayed staring at his fingers, confused. I felt guilty for getting older, for leaving him behind; it was hard to think of what to say. Then I had an idea. I reached into my bedside drawer for my wallet, and carefully took out a photograph that I keep.

'See,' I said. 'Do you remember?'

He climbed beside me on the bed, his feet not quite able to reach the floor. He kicked his legs excitedly, 'At the zoo! At the zoo!'

'That's right. See. I'm a tiger too.'

We went to Bristol Zoo for my sixth birthday party and had our faces painted. Nanny Noo took the photograph of us, our cheeks pressed together, we're both roaring at the camera. She carried it in her purse for years, but when I once mentioned it was my favourite she insisted that I took it. There was no arguing with her, she absolutely insisted.

I had something else in my wallet too, but I didn't want to show him it. I didn't want to build his hopes up in case things didn't work out. It was a folded sheet of paper, tucked away behind my cash card. The ward receptionist had printed it off the Internet for me a few days before. She was a nice lady, forever chewing gum, proudly chatting to the cleaners about her daughter; the latest piano grade she was going for, how she was a talented tap dancer too.

I'd waited for a lull in their conversation, which didn't come. She didn't even pause for breath before turning to me and asking, 'Can I help you with anything, lovely?'

'I need an address,' I said. 'Can you look something up for me on the computer?'

'Uh-huh.'

'Um— It's a holiday park. A caravan park. I can't remember where it is exactly. I think it's in—'

'What's it called, lovely?'

'Sorry. Yeah. It's called Ocean Cove. Well, it used to be. I suppose it might have—'

Her long red fingernails were already tapping at the keys, quick as a machine gun. 'Ocean Cove Holiday Park in Portland, Dorset. Is that the one?'

———

Dad drove the Ford Mondeo Estate, with Mum feeding him crisps and bites of apple.

Simon was asleep, with a Transformer hugging his knees. I played on my Game Boy until the batteries died. Then we played a game of who would be first to See the Sea. My parents let me win. Mum blew a kiss into the rear-view mirror.

Dad pressed the button to open the sunroof. He said how good salt air made him feel.

As we rolled over a speed bump at the entrance gate, Simon was shaken awake. His eyes widened, he clapped his hands, unable, as always, to find the right words.

———

'Is that the one, lovely?'

'Yes. That's it. That's where—'

She clicked her mouse and Google spat the address out, with a small grainy map.

If she'd asked what I wanted with it, perhaps I would have told her the truth. This is where I abandoned my brother, and it's where he needs me the most.

Maybe that would have shaken her from her trance; she'd tilt her head sympathetically and say, 'I'll tell you what, lovely. Why don't you wait here a minute and I'll go and see if any of the nurses are free to have a chat with you?'

But she didn't do that,

because

this

was

something

that

all   the

STARS

in

the

entire

UNIVERSE

had planned for me, and because as I folded the sheet of paper into my wallet she was already explaining to the cleaner how her daughter was seriously thinking about ballet classes too, but there were only so many days in the week.

I jolted bolt upright. The rainbows had gone, so had Simon. Claire-or-maybe-Anna was standing in my doorway. 'I've booked us a taxi,' she was saying. 'It should be here in twenty minutes.'

I rubbed at my face with both hands. There was a damp patch of dribble on my pillow. 'I think someone's been asleep again,' Claire-or-maybe-Anna said. 'You get yourself dressed. It's a beautiful day, feels like spring might be saying hello at last. I'll give you a shout when the taxi's here.'

I splashed my face in cold water and rummaged through the pile of clothes on my bedroom floor. I picked out my green combat trousers and camouflage jacket. I don't want to be in the army or anything. I was just going through a phase of wearing the gear, to make myself feel less afraid.

I sat back on the bed to lace my boots. 'I know you're still under there, Si.'

He was never any good at keeping quiet. It was like when we used to hide behind the door waiting for Dad. As I shut the door, he broke out in a fit of giggles.

Claire-or-maybe-Anna thanked the taxi driver and told him some-one from the ward would ring when we needed picking up. In the waiting room the dentist appeared, a hygiene mask clinging tightly to her chin on stretched elastic straps.

'Matthew Homes,' she called.

I turned to Claire-or-maybe-Anna, 'I'd rather go in by myself, if that's okay?'

She hesitated a moment. 'Um. Sure. I'll wait here.'

I told the dentist I'd be right through. I just needed to go to the loo quickly. 'We're along the corridor, second on the right,' she explained. 'Come through when you're ready.'

There's no security at dental surgeries, nobody watching the doors or strutting around with bunches of keys and red clip-boards. As it happens, I was registered with my own dentist. But the Emergency Clinic is nearer to the train station.

When your big brother is calling, when it's finally time to go and play, if you need to escape from a psychiatric ward – the first thing to do is observe. Then get the hard work done for you. *Say, Ahh.* I'm a mental patient, not an idiot.

sharp scratch

Denise wasn't best pleased when I came in for my injection the other day, unwashed and hungover.

'You smell of beer, Matt.'

'It's not illegal.'

She shook her head and let out a tired sigh, 'No. It's not illegal.'

We'd gone through to the small clinic/let's-talk-about-how-you're-feeling-in-yourself room at the end of the top corridor; the one that always smells strongly of disinfectant. That doesn't help. I can get a bit panicky at injection times and the disinfectant smell definitely doesn't help.

Denise opened her bag of tricks and I asked if I could have a drink of water. She gestured to the sink, 'Help yourself.'

I picked up a mug with the complicated name of a medication stamped across the side, and a slogan about *Treating Today for Tomorrow*. They're handed out to places like this by visiting drug companies. Last time I went in the office to borrow the Nursing Dictionary, I counted three mugs, a mouse mat, a bunch of pens, two Post-it note booklets and the wall clock – all sporting the brands of different medicines. It's like being in prison and having to look at adverts for fucking locks. That's what I should have said too, because it's a good point I reckon. But I never think of these things until after.

I gulped back the water and poured myself a second mug. Denise was watching me closely. 'I was up drinking with The Pig,' I explained. As if me wanting two mugs of tap water needed an explanation. 'We had a couple this morning too.'

'Really, Matt. You're your own worst enemy.'

That's a strange thing to say to someone with a serious mental disease. Of course I'm my own worst enemy. That's the whole problem. I should have said that too. Except maybe not, because she looked tired. She looked upset as well. And usually she might give me a little lecture, but this time she didn't. She didn't lecture me. You could tell by the way she let out another sigh that she wasn't going to lecture me. It was a sigh that said: Not today. Today we'll just get through this.

'I'm afraid I've some very disappointing news,' she said.

I told you there was a strange atmosphere, didn't I? I said how you could cut it with a knife. How you could cut it with the crappy blunt scissors they give us in Art Group.

Denise is a woman, which means she can multi-task. That's what they say, isn't it? That's the kind of blah blah blah people drivel.

'It's about Hope Road,' she said. 'It looks like we may have to scale back the groups, maybe scaling back on everything.'

'Oh right.'

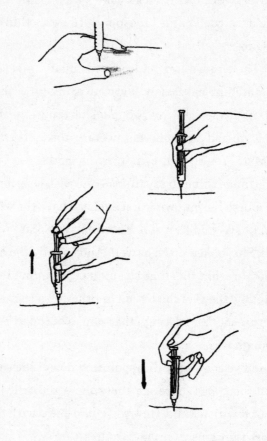

'We've been fighting it for a while. But services are being cut right across the Trust. Right across the NHS really. And, well, it seems we're no exception.'

She was looking at me to respond so what I said was, 'Is your job safe?'

She smiled at me then, but she still looked sad. 'You're very sweet. It's probably safe, yes. But as I say, we will be scaling back. It's all taken us a bit off guard to be honest. There's some consultations due later this week. But it doesn't look— Well, we've decided to start letting service users know, so it isn't such a shock.'

'Who?'

'Service Users. Um— Patients.'

'Oh. Right.'

They have a bunch of names for us. Service Users must be the latest. I think there must be people who get paid to decide this shit.

I thought about Steve. He's definitely the sort to say Service User. He'd say it like he deserved a knighthood for being all sensitive and empowering. Then I imagined him losing his job – and to be honest, that caught *me* off guard. I don't hate these people. I just hate not having the choice to get rid of them.

'What about Steve? Is he—'

'Well, I don't really want to get into all that. It isn't my place. I just wanted to let you know about—'

She trailed off, and I couldn't tell if it was because she was upset, or just concentrating. Perhaps she had to concentrate not to be upset. 'Are you okay?' I asked. 'Do you want some water?'

'No, no. I'm fine. It's just a real blow for us.'

She took a deep breath and let it all out slowly, like with the breathing exercises they get us to do. Practise what you preach, I guess. Then she kind of launched into a script. She said all this stuff that you could tell she'd been saying to everyone. About how whatever way things went, she'd still be working with me. She'd still see me at home and help with my forms and budgeting and that kind of thing. And we could still meet in the cafe that we sometimes meet in. Or go to the supermarket together. Then she finished with this bit about how capable and independent she knew I could be – that she has every faith in me. I'm not saying it wasn't a nice script. I'm just saying it was a script.

But then I think she slipped off the page, because in all the time I've known Denise I've never once heard her swear. She's a very calm person. I guess she needs to be. I've never known her get rattled or lose her composure, but as she drew up the syringe, her hands shaking a little, I heard her say under her breath. 'This effing government.'

That's exactly how she said it too. She said *effing*. I never knew people said that for real. It was almost sadder in a way. I didn't like seeing her like that. I don't like seeing anyone upset. I'm just no good at comforting people. I did think about reaching out to touch her arm, but what if she pulled away? And I could have said it would all be okay, but how could I know that?

And anyway, we're not really on the same side are we? I reckon that's why she decided I was taking the piss, when she turned to see me smiling. It was an awkward smile, but you only really know what a smile means when you own the face behind it. Everyone else just sees the smile they expect it to be.

'Look,' she snapped. 'I know you don't like it here.'

'I don't mind it.'

'Sometimes you do. And that's fine. But it's a good service that helps a lot of people.'

That was unkind of her. Making me out to be the bad guy. Whatever side she thinks I'm on, it ain't me threatening to close the place down. Strangely enough they don't let us Service Users decide that sort of thing.

'Anyway,' she said. Back to her usual calm. 'I just wanted to let you know. It's all a bit up in the air, but things could happen very quickly. Money seems to be making all the decisions these days. It's largely out of our hands.'

I looked at the syringe, at the glistening needle. 'How much does that stuff cost?'

'It's different, Matt. This is what keeps you out of hospital, and keeps you well. And it'll be even more important if other support is withdrawn.'

'Would you care to see my arse, Denise?'

That made her chuckle. It'd been getting a bit tense, but that took the edge off. We do get on okay sometimes. She did this pretend coy act, picking up a slip of paper and using it like an old-fashioned fan. Like you see ladies use in period TV dramas. 'Mr Homes. How can a girl resist?'

I undid my belt and let my jeans drop to my ankles, then I pulled down the back of my pants and she knelt on the floor behind me.

I guess you don't see that in the dramas. I have a few compliance problems with tablets, the answer – a long, sharp needle. Every other week, alternate sides. I'm telling you, they use me like an effing pin cushion.

'Okay. Sharp scratch.'

I had to steady myself, resting a hand on the counter, swallowing hard, forcing back the urge to throw up.

'Nearly there,' she said.

She swabbed the puncture wound with a wad of cotton wool, and pressed on a plaster.

It's hard to know what to say afterwards. This time I had a question though. 'Will I still get to use the computer?'

Denise dropped the used needle into a special plastic bucket, snapping the lip closed.

'I honestly don't know, Matt. It's all completely up in the air. The last thing I heard there was talk of subletting half the building to a graphics design company! You use it a lot, don't you?'

'What?'

'The computer.'

'A bit. Only when nobody else wants it.'

'I wasn't criticizing. It's great to know you're making use of it. It would be wonderful to read something you've written, if you'd ever let—'

'Can I have that?'

'Sorry?'

I was pointing to the slip of paper that she'd used as a pretend fan.

'Um— If you want, by all means. It's just the Instruction Sheet though. It's for nurses really. I can get you a Patient Information one if you'd prefer?'

'Patient? I thought we were Service Users.'

'Well— Yes.'

'Graphic designers, did you say?'

She shrugged, 'It's been suggested. Nothing is definite. As I said, they'll be some more consultations and I'll speak with you again as soon as we know more. But the important thing to take away from this is that you'll still be getting support. Okay?'

As I left I opened up the slip of paper and pointed to the pictures; neat little line drawings, a step by step guide.

'I guess we need graphic designers too, eh?'

Denise rolled her eyes at me, but in a friendly sort of way. We do get on okay sometimes. 'That's one way of looking at it,' she said. 'Now you go home and get some rest.'

SCHIZOPHRENIA n. a severe mental disorder
characterized by a disintegration in the
process of thinking, of contact with reality,
and of emotional responsiveness. Etymology:
From the Greek Skhizein ('to split') and Phren
('mind').

When I look at the photograph of Simon and me at
Bristol Zoo, with our faces painted like tigers, I look
at myself, but do not see myself.

I know that he is me because I am told he is me,
but I do not remember turning six years old, going to
Bristol Zoo, having my face painted like a tiger, and
smiling into the lens of a camera. I do not remember
my brother's face pressed against my face, the black
stripes smudging into the orange on our cheeks.

If I look closely I can see we have the same colour
eyes, not me and Simon, but me and the boy who is also
me, the boy who I can no longer recognize, with whom I
no longer share a single thought, worry, or hope.

We are the same person, all that separates us is
the passing of time. There is an unbreakable thread
connecting us, but I do not know him any more.

I am me. I am in my flat, sitting on the chair with
the blistered arms. I have a cigarette between my lips,

and this typewriter balanced on my lap. It's heavy. I
can feel the weight of it, it's uncomfortable, and soon
I may move position, or place the typewriter on my
table, and sit on the wooden chair. This is me, this is
what is happening right now, but in the place in my
head where pictures form, I am seeing another me.

It's a bright afternoon, the first taste of spring.
I felt safer outdoors, off the train. It wasn't the
noise of the baby so much, but when a baby cries on a
train other passengers share irritated glances. Too
much small print. I'd stayed in the space between two
carriages for most of the journey, occasionally going
into the toilet to smoke.

'Are you lost, young man?'

I had been following road signs, but at the mini
roundabout by the furthest edge of the marina, a sign
was missing. There were roadworks; traffic cones, men
with hard hats and yellow jackets, a pneumatic drill
making it impossible to think. I hadn't noticed the
white-haired lady, waiting patiently for the green
man to flash so she could safely cross. She smelled
of perfumed soap. I could smell her through the oily
stink of fresh tarmac.

I was looking at the grainy map that the ward
secretary had printed for me, trying to make sense of
it. I tried to sound normal and relaxed. 'Um, yeah. I'm
heading to Portland. Do you know the way?'

She held a walking stick, pinned with silver badges from places like Land's End and The Lake District. She leant closer and the stick wobbled, 'You'll have to speak up, I'm afraid.'

'No,' I said. 'Don't worry. I'm not lost.'

'It's a lovely afternoon, isn't it?' It was still cold enough to wear a pullover, but the sky was as clear as the water. That's the way she put it, anyway. Along the harbour wall fishermen stood as still as statues, bait writhing in the dirty Tupperware at their feet.

'Did you say Portland?' the lady asked suddenly, in that way people do when actually they had heard all along.

I nodded, yes.

I've always written stories, right back from when I was really little. My first attempts were terrible, but when I got a bit older, and was imprisoned at the kitchen table, with a stack of Key-Stage English workbooks, a word processor, and a mad mother, they started getting better. I wrote about magic and monsters and mysterious lands where adventures happen.

I've never stopped.

The old lady's face wrinkled in thought. There's a coastal footpath from Weymouth to Portland, she explained. Along the Rodwell Trail. It's a Dead Railway. The tracks were pulled up years ago, but the platforms remain, overgrown with weeds and brambles. She gave

me directions, explaining with a wave of her stick
that I could join the path a short way along from the
Asda Petrol Station. 'It's a beautiful walk,' she said.
'And Portland, it's so lovely. May I ask what's taking
you?'

'No. Thanks for the directions.'

It was a beautiful walk. I bought a cheese and ham
sandwich and a packet of Skittles from the Asda garage,
and ate them on Chesil Beach.

I thought of Simon's keepsake box, how his pebbles
clattered at the bottom. He would collect the shiniest
stones and pieces of eroded glass from shallow waters.
Dad told him it was best to leave them, they never look
half as impressive when they're dry, but Simon could
never resist.

I searched through my pockets and rolled a cigarette.
I can't blow smoke rings, but I can do something much
better. I took a deep lungful, holding my breath as
long as I could. Then I slowly blew it out and watched
his face appear. 'Alright, Si.'

'Hi Matthew.'

He wasn't a tiger this time. He was older, his hair
combed neatly for a school photo day. This was around
the time I'd called him a baby for having a comfort
blanket. He was pretending to still be cross.

'Give me a break, Simon. I'm coming, aren't I?'

'Are you, Matt? Are you coming to play with me?'

I picked up a pebble and skimmed it into the sea. The cloud of smoke dispersed. 'Yeah, I'm coming. We're going to play forever.'

Chesil Beach curves like a spine from the Dorset mainland to the west coast of Portland. Ocean Cove is on the east coast. I still had a way to go, but my brother carried me.

In the window of Portland Tophill library, a book caught my eye. It was in the children's section, where there is a miniature plastic table and chairs. How can I deal with... WHEN PEOPLE DIE?

The librarian told me they were about to close. I said I wouldn't be long. I sat on the Space Rocket carpet and read about what death is. When someone's body stops working and can't be made better, the book explained. Dead people can't feel pain or know what's going on. I read about Wes who is angry with his brother Denny for leaving him on his own, and making his mum and dad unhappy. It had pictures and everything.

Shadows crept slowly across the bookshelves. The weather was turning; drizzly raindrops slapped at the window. I might have outstayed my welcome. The librarian appeared, raising a hand to her mouth, letting out two polite coughs. I asked how far it was to Ocean Cove. 'About twenty minutes,' she said. 'Maybe

twenty-five. It's easy enough though, straight along
the coastal road. Pity it's raining. Did you want to
take the book out?'

'It's for kids,' I said.

'We're closing,' she said.

WELCOME TO OCEAN COVE
HOLIDAY PARK, the sign said.

There were no tents pitched, and the caravans stood
empty, silently awaiting the arrival of the season's
first holidaymakers. It was unnervingly quiet. In the
whole park, only a single caravan showed any sign of
life – a warm glow behind closed curtains. It was a way
along the path, towards the top end of the site.

I felt myself drawn towards it, moving quietly,
keeping to the edge of the footpath, where I wouldn't
be seen.

Up close, I could hear a murmur of voices coming
from inside. Then I started to imagine something. It
was only my imagination, but in some ways it was more
like a dream because I couldn't control it, or choose
to stop thinking it: This was the caravan that we had
stayed in, and the people who I could hear talking were
my mum and dad. We were still on our holiday, like time
had somehow got trapped. The whole rest of the world
had moved on, but here it couldn't let go. In the warm

light, in the murmured voices, the past was repeating
itself.

Simon and I were tucked up in our beds, Mum and
Dad were settling into their evening. Dad was reading
out crossword clues, then they would both fall silent,
thinking, until Mum got distracted and said, 'Matthew
wasn't himself today.'

'No?'

'This afternoon, he was white as a sheet.'

'I didn't notice anything.'

'You weren't here. You were flying the kite with
Simon, I tried to persuade him to join you, but he
wouldn't. And, oh I don't know. He said he was playing
hide-and-seek but-'

A tightness knotted in my chest, dropping into the
pit of my tummy. This is the night it happens, this
is our last night. Dad folds away the paper, placing
down his wine glass. Mum leans into him, draping an
arm across his chest. One of them says, 'Do you think
we were too hard on him?'

'When?'

'The other day. It was a nasty fall. I wouldn't be
surprised if that knee scars. He didn't need us to tell
him off too.'

'He should know better-'

'But they're boys. Aren't they supposed to misbehave a
bit? Besides, they both knew they weren't allowed down

there. We can't keep putting all the blame on Matt.'

This wasn't a memory, it wasn't a conversation I'd ever overheard. This was plain wishful thinking. 'He still feels terrible that Simon had to carry him,' Mum was saying. 'He mentioned that too. You know how he can be, when he blames himself for things. He goes around in circles. It breaks my heart.'

'Let's have a nice day with them both tomorrow. We'll let Matt decide what we do. I'll have a chat with him at some point, see if there's anything on his mind.'

'Honestly, Richard. He was ashen.'

The rain was soaking to my skin. It was getting darker. I stepped around the side of the caravan, towards our bedroom.

I tapped on the window.

'What was that?'

'What?'

They were different voices now, clearer voices.

'I'm sure I heard something.'

The curtains twitched, I turned quickly away. It wasn't Mum and Dad in there. It wasn't us. I rushed past the shower blocks, the recycling bins, the water tap.

It was all so familiar.

I pushed my hands deep into my pockets and strode up the narrow path, out of the side gate, then along the short stretch of main road and down onto the winding cliff path. The wind was picking up, it was getting colder. Branches rustled noisily over my head. I looked up and nearly slipped on some wet leaves. I guess that was important; it kept him near.

With each careful step I felt him more closely. Everything was exactly as I remembered, until I turned the corner, to where it had actually happened, and here it was different. The rusting handrail, the weather-beaten sign. This was his legacy:

Children must be accompanied by an adult
AT ALL TIMES

The handrail felt cold to the touch. I ducked beneath it, scrambling through a patch of damp nettles, up the steep dirt bank. Then I took shuffling sideways steps, until I reached the very edge of the cliff.

The edge of my world.

Somewhere the last of the evening sun was dropping into the sea. But not here. There are no sunsets in the east. No spectacular endings alight with colour. In the east, day simply fades into unremarkable blackness. That felt right. He'd been lonely long enough. I closed my eyes, and summoned the courage to take my final step.

But in the place in my head where pictures form I was seeing another me, a nine-year-old boy who was now opening his eyes, who had woken in the dead of night with thoughts, worries, and hopes I no longer shared.

Perhaps my nine-year-old self could remember the six-year-old, perhaps he could still remember how the tiger paints smelled, and the smiling face of Nanny Noo, half obscured behind her camera.

I do not have a split mind. I am not different people. I am myself, the same self I have always been, the one person I can never escape. I am sitting in my living room, tugging at the thread of time, so that I am standing on the cliff edge and tugging at the thread of time, so that I am waking up in our caravan, my thoughts moving in circles around the little girl with her cloth doll, the way she shouted at me, telling me I'd ruined everything, even though I only wanted to help.

'Wake up, Simon. Wake up.' I was speaking in a whisper, so as not to wake my parents through the thin walls. 'Wake up.'

I reached across the short void between our two beds and prodded him, my fingers sinking into the soft fat of his belly. He blinked twice, then opened his eyes wide.

'What is it Matt? Is it morning?'

'No.'

'Why are you awake?'

'I can't sleep. Do you want to see something?'

'What?'

'Do you want to see a dead body?'

'What? Yeah!'

'I'm serious.'

He shuffled to the edge of his bed and thrust his head across the gap, towards me. 'No you're not.'

'Yes I am.'

At that, he let out a yelp of laughter and threw his head back onto his pillow.

'Shut up, Si. You'll wake 'em up. Why do you have to be so noisy all the time?'

'Sorry. I didn't-'

'Keep your voice down. Get dressed.'

Mum or Dad coughed in their sleep, and we both froze. Simon made a show of it, making his whole body rigid, only his eyes moving from side to side, grinning at me.

'Stop being stupid. Here, put this on.'

I threw him a handful of clothes, and his raincoat with the toggles.

'It's not raining out, Matt.'

'No, but it might. And it's cold. Where's the torch?'

'It's in your bag, not my bag.'

'Oh yeah. Shhh.'

We dressed, and he put on his raincoat, then started fumbling with the toggles. He was always fumbling with the toggles when he got nervous or excited about something. He hated it if anyone tried to help, so I

watched him, flicking the torch on and off whilst he
put his toggles in the wrong holes, and started again.

'I can't do my toggles, Matt.'

'Do you want me to help?'

'No. I can do it. Are we really going to see a dead
body?'

'Yeah. Put that one in there.'

'I can do it.'

'Shhh. Fine. I was only-'

'Done it!' He smiled at me, his big daft grin.

'Come on then. Let's go.'

I can see my hand reaching to the door handle of
the caravan, but I do not recognize it. I cannot see
the thread of time that turned that child's hands into
these hands; tobacco-stained, ink-stained, nails bitten
to frustrated stubs.

I opened the door, and stepped into the last half-
hour of my brother's life. He followed, breathless with
excitement.

'Where are we going? Where is it?'

'It isn't far, up here.'

'I can feel some rain.'

'Pull your hood up then.'

We didn't need the torch until we were past the
caravans, and onto the narrow road leading towards
the place where you stood if it was your turn to close
your eyes and count to a hundred.

The rain started falling harder. Simon was trailing now, looking over his shoulder. 'We should go back, Matthew. I'm tired. We're not supposed to be out at night. Nobody's awake. Let's go back.'

'Don't be a baby all the time. It's around this side. Here. Hold this.'

I thrust the torch at him, and led us round the side of the camping shop, to the patch of overgrown grass near to the recycling bins. It was darker there.

I felt afraid, perhaps.

I probably felt afraid because at night-time everything is more frightening, but more than that, I felt angry. I felt angry that I was always responsible for everything, how Simon got all the attention, that I'd been shouted at when I fell and hurt my knee, and I felt angry that the girl with her stupid doll had thought that she could shout at me too.

I felt angry with Simon for not holding the torch still, for the way he shifted his weight from foot to foot, whining that it was time to go back, that he didn't want to see a dead body. I pushed my hands into the wet soil where the wooden cross was placed, until the tips of my fingers reached something soft.

'I don't like it any more, Matthew. I'm getting wet. There isn't a dead body there. I'm going back. I'm going back now.'

'Wait! Hold the torch still, hold it down here.'

I pulled away a handful of mud, and another. With Simon beside me wiping rain from his cheeks. He wanted me to stop, he was frightened. I didn't stop. I lifted her into the air, she was dirty, sodden, her arms flopped at her sides. I held her, and began to laugh, laughing at Simon for being so pathetic; 'It's a doll Simon, it's just a stupid doll, Look! Look! She wants to play with you.'

He was backing away, clutching his chest in the way he did when panic took hold, when no words could calm him down. He was begging me, Stop! Stop! STOP! His trembling hands holding the torch, pointing it at the doll. Her button eyes glistened in the beam.

'She wants to play with you, Simon. She wants to play chase.'

He tried to run, his stupid way of running, hunched right forwards with his legs wide apart, lumbering through the gap between the shop and the recycling bins.

'She wants to play.'

I looped behind the water tap, leaping into his path, cutting off the route back to the caravans. He froze, dropping the torch. It clattered on the ground. I picked it up, still laughing, and shone it to see his face.

It wasn't funny now. It stopped being funny. He was full of tears, strings of snot dripping from his nose, clinging to his wet lips. He didn't look like the moon any more. He looked terrified.

In the distance waves crashed against the cliffs, and somewhere, the girl, the girl who had shouted at me, who had told me I wasn't welcome any more, somewhere she whimpered in her sleep.

'Simon. I was joking. It was a joke.'

'NO, NO!' He punched me in my stomach, as hard as he could.

I was always such a wimp. My body crumpled, I couldn't get my breath back.

'It was-'

I couldn't catch my breath.

He turned, heading along the path, away from the caravans, away from me. 'Simon, wait. Please.'

But he was faster now, reaching the side entrance, onto the main road, down onto the cliff path, into darkness.

'Simon, wait.'

I couldn't reach him.

I couldn't.

The end of Simon Anthony Homes was cruel and sudden.

It was dismissive.

That's how I think of it now. It was the whole universe turning its back and walking away, incapable of caring.

He didn't fall far, or particularly hard. It was no harder than I had fallen only a few days before.

And at the exact same spot; the same twist in the path where exposed roots snare unsuspecting ankles. There was the shock of the fall and the blood on my knee and Simon had carried me. He carried me all the way to safety, all by himself, because he loved me.

The difference – a difference – was that in the moment before Simon fell, he turned. He glanced back over his shoulder to look at me. It was the briefest moment.

'Talk to me.'

It happened so fast and I can never slow it down.

I don't know why I should expect to. But I do, in a way. I am a selfish person and I feel cheated out of the sensation that you sometimes hear people describe, when they talk about how the enormity of a situation made everything appear to move in slow motion.

It wasn't like that.

'Please. Say something.'

He had turned back to look at me, and I try to convince myself that he was smiling. That the joke was on me. He wasn't scared at all. It was all a game, and he was happy because for once it was me who was tricked. Or else I tell myself it was a look of forgiveness. In the final moment, he knew that I loved him, and I would never want to hurt him.

But it happened too fast. My world didn't move in slow motion. I sometimes wonder if his did, and if so, what lasting final image did I offer? Did it give him any comfort, or only betrayal?

It was the way he landed, his neck still turning. It was the weakness in his muscle tone, a symptom of his disorder. It was a chance in a million, a grubby statistic. It was the movement of his body, the speed, the trajectory, the slipperiness of the rain-soaked earth, the exact and stubborn location of an exposed root.

And it was me.

Whatever wave had been swelling in the sea in the seconds before he fell, would break in the seconds after. This dismissive and uncaring universe simply carried on with its business, as if nothing of any consequence had happened.

'Please. Talk to me.'

I am trying to lift him, to carry him, but the ground is wet. There is mud in my mouth, in my eyes, and the rain keeps falling. I lift him and fall, lift him and fall. He is silent. I am begging him to say something. Please, say something. I fall again, landing hard against a rock, and I am holding him, holding his face to mine, so close I can feel his warmth leave. Please. Please. Talk to me.

'I can't carry you. I'm sorry.'

The little cloth doll is lying beside us in the mud.

She looks cold without her coat. I gently, ever so gently, lift Simon's head, and place her beneath it. I want to make him comfortable.

I am me. I am in my flat, sitting on the chair with the blistered arms. It's getting late. I have been typing for a long time, and am tired. I've stubbed a cigarette out on my forearm. That's blistered too. I hoped the pain might keep me here, but I can't grip the thread.

Time falls through my fingers.

In the place in my head where pictures form, I'm seeing another me. I have run away from a psychiatric ward, am standing on a cliff top at the farthest edge of my world. It's dark now, but the moon is bright. Big too. That's Simon, watching me. I can hear his voice in the wind. He's cold, he can't do his toggles up. I shuffle forward, pushing my toecaps over the edge.

'Are you listening?'

I imagine how it must be to die, to be dead. What would happen to my body, how would my family find out? Who would tell Nanny Noo? Who would tell Jacob? It makes me feel guilty to think like this. I need courage to take the final step.

'Come away from there.'

There is someone behind me, I can hear footsteps. 'Are you even listening? It's dangerous. You might fall.'

But in the place in my head where pictures form,

I am seeing another me; a nine-year-old boy at the foot of his parents' bed, muddy rainwater dripping from his clothes into a puddle on the lino floor. He is watching his parents, the way they hold each other in their sleep, the way his mother's face is pressed awkwardly into the nook of his father's arm, her mouth wide open, hair from his armpit brushing against her forehead, the sheets bunched up at their feet, their ankles not quite touching.

This boy knows he must wake them. If he listens he will hear me, shouting to him: Wake them up. Tell them. There was an accident, Simon has fallen. Something terrible has happened.

Wake them up.

The boy presses his back to the wall, slides silently to the floor, hugging knees to chest, hearing only the last few raindrops tapping at the window and the occasional murmur from his parents, as they hold each other in their sleep.

'Matthew, sweetheart. What's happened?' Mum knelt beside me, shaking me awake. The room was bright with dawn sunshine. I could feel the heat of her breath against my cheek, the faint smell of decay.

In a few minutes my dad would be pacing outside, calling for my brother. Telling him to stop messing about. The sound of sirens in the distance playing a

tune to the fear in Mum's voice. 'Don't just look at me.
Talk to me. What have you done? Where's Simon?'

My neck felt tight, stiff from being on the floor,
from a night in damp clothes. I started to shiver, my
teeth chattering uncontrollably.

'I'm really cold, Mummy.'

'Forget being cold. Where's Simon?'

I didn't go to the hospital with them. I stayed with Mr
and Mrs Onslow, a retired couple who owned the caravan
next to ours.

'We've Snakes and Ladders,' said Mrs Onslow, placing
a tray of squash and biscuits on the carpet beside me.
I didn't respond. She went back to the small kitchen
area to busy herself with dishes. I guess she didn't
know what else to say.

There was a knock at the door, and Mr Onslow
folded his newspaper. I could make out Dad's voice in
their whispered exchange, but I couldn't hear what was
said.

Dad came through to join me. He sat on the carpet
cross-legged like I was, which was strange because I'd
never seen him sit that way, so wondered why he chose
to now. He looked tired and pale.

'Alright mon ami. How you doing?' he asked, ruffling
my hair.

I shrugged.

'The police are here-' His voice cracked and trailed off. He paused, composing himself. 'It won't take long. You need to tell them what you told us.'

I looked hard at the floor.

'I thought I woke you up, Dad.'

Mum hugged me so tight I thought my ribs might crack. She needed to make sure I was really there. I was conscious of the two policemen awkwardly nursing mugs of tea, so as soon as she relaxed her grip I pulled away.

The policemen introduced themselves.

One of them was about Dad's age and had a bushy ginger-brown moustache and glasses. The other was younger, with slicked-back black hair, sticking up a little in the middle. They both wore uniform, their hats on the table.

'The first thing to say is you're not in any trouble,' said moustache. 'Nobody is accusing you of anything, nobody is saying you've done anything wrong.'

Mum squeezed my hand.

'We need to take a statement from you, which means I'm going to ask you some questions and we're going to write down what you tell us. But if you want to stop at any point you can just say. What do you need to do if you want to stop?'

'Say.'

'That's right. Okay, now before we start, I'm going to tell you a story. Do you like stories?'

'Sometimes.'

'Sometimes. Well, I'm not good at stories, but this one isn't very long. Once upon a time there was a boy of about your age, perhaps a bit older, and he decided to try smoking. So he took a cigarette from his dad's pack and started to smoke it in his bedroom. Then he heard his mum coming up the stairs so he quickly put it out. She came in his room and asked, have you been smoking? And the boy said no. So that's the story, and I did tell you I wasn't good at stories. But tell me, was the boy lying or was he telling the truth?'

'Lying.'

'He was lying. That's right. Why do you think he lied?'

'So he wouldn't get in trouble.'

'That's what I think too. But if you remember, you're not in trouble, and you haven't done anything wrong. So I need you to tell the truth, okay?'

I felt an emptiness filling my chest, and thought it might swallow me whole.

'But if you don't remember something, or don't know, then you must say you don't know. What colour's my front door?'

'I don't know.'

'That's right. You don't know. You haven't seen it, so you don't know. Is it yellow?'

'I don't know.'

'Good. Now remind me what you need to do if you want us to stop?'

'Say.'

'Exactly.'

He sucked air between his teeth, and nodded to slicked-back black hair, who bit the lid off his pen. 'I've done a lot of talking, haven't I? Let's give you a turn. I want you to tell me about last night.'

I expected to be placed in handcuffs and sent to prison immediately, but that didn't happen. After they left I waited for my parents to shout at me, but that didn't happen either.

I expected it because I was too stupid to understand that some things are too big. Any punishment is an insult to the crime.

This voice – his voice – do you hear it inside your head, or does it seem to come from the outside, and what exactly does it say, and does it tell you to do things, or just comment on what you're doing already, and have you done any of the things it says, which things, you said your mum takes tablets, what are they for, is anyone else in your family FUCKING MAD, and do you use illicit drugs, how much alcohol do you drink, every week, every day, and how are you feeling in yourself right now, on

a scale of 1-10, and what about on a scale of 1-7,400,000,
000,000,000,000,000,000,000, and how is your sleep of late,
and what of your appetite, and what exactly did happen
that night on the cliff edge, in your own words, do you
remember, can you remember, do you have any questions?

No.

You said your brother was in the moon, you said you
could hear him in the wind?

Yes.

What was he saying?

I don't remember.

Was he telling you to jump? Was he telling you to
kill yourself?

It's not like that, don't say it like that. He wanted
me to play with him. He's lonely, that's all.

We're not trying to upset you, but it's important we
talk about this.

Why?

We need to know that you're safe. You say he wanted
you to play with him. How do you play with a dead
person, Matt?

Fuck off.

Somewhere in all the paperwork that follows me
around is my Risk Assessment. Bright yellow paper
shouting warnings about how fragile and vulnerable
and dangerous I am.

Name: Matthew Homes
DoB: 12.05.1990
Diagnosis: The Slithery Snake
Current Medication(s): The Works

Risk to Self/Others (please provide vague, embellished examples presented as hard fact): Matthew lives alone, has a limited support network and few friends. He suffers from command hallucinations, which he attributes to a dead sibling. Crazy shit, eh? Problem is he's been known to interpret said hallucinations as an invite to off himself.

He is currently managed by Brunel Community Mental Health Team, and sporadically attends therapeutic groups at Hope Rd Day Centre (or else he sits alone in his flat, tapping away endlessly on a typewriter his grandmother gave him, which if you think about it, is a bit mental in itself).

On 2nd April 2008, a few weeks into a lengthy hospital admission on Crazy Crazy NutsNuts ward, Matthew went AWOL. He revisited the site where his brother had died, with a view to committing the last hurrah.

This attempt was foiled by an anonymous Passerby. Matthew does not appear to present a significant risk to others. That said, when the Passerby later contacted the ward – seemingly concerned about Matt's well-being and seeking assurances that he had returned safely

– staff were able to press upon her how frightened she must have been, and indeed, how she had feared for her very life.

So, you know. Can't be too careful.

> Fuck off the
> lot of you.

Someone was touching my arm.

I turned around quickly, nearly losing balance. Her grip tightened. 'Jesus,' she said. 'I thought– I thought you were going to fall. Are you okay?'

She had red hair. It blew across her face, long strands escaping from beneath the hood of a raincoat. I could just make out her freckles in the moonlight. And held tight to her chest – like the beating of her heart depended on it – was Simon's comfort blanket.

This made sense. It made the perfect sense of a dream before waking. In this dream she was Bianca from EastEnders, and she had brought me Simon's blanket to keep him warm. I reached to take it, but now she was moving away from me – still looking at me – reaching behind her to feel the safety of the handrail.

'It's mine,' she said.

'But–'

There was something different. She lifted the scrap

of yellow cloth to her chin and I could now see a black plastic buckle. There was a sleeve, a collar. It wasn't his blanket. She wasn't Bianca.

'It's- It's you,' I said. 'I know you.'

I forget how intimidating I can be. She looked at my camouflage jacket, my big black boots. 'I don't know you,' she said. Her voice sounded small. 'I was just checking you're okay, that's all. I'm going home now.'

'You kept it. You've kept it this whole time.'

Simon was in the movement of her hair. He was in the little yellow coat as it billowed in the wind.

'I'll leave you to it,' she said.

'I can't remember your name?'

'That's because you don't know me.'

She quickly turned to leave, but I couldn't let her. I had to be sure she was real.

'Let go of me!'

The little coat dropped to the ground, gathered straight away by a rogue gust of wind. Simon could be sneaky. I moved after him, getting a foot on it just in time. 'Got it,' I smiled.

I thought she'd be pleased, but she looked frightened now. Really frightened. 'Please, why are you doing this? I don't know you. I only wanted to help-'

I was holding her, that was the problem. I was gripping hold of her wrist. 'No. You don't understand. I'm not going to hurt you. I never meant to hurt you.'

As she pulled away I let go of her wrist, causing her to stumble to the ground. And in that moment I saw her as a small child again, as a little girl tending to a tiny grave. I had only ever wanted to help her, to make it better, but I didn't know how. I'd hovered awkwardly, unsure of what to do. I'd wanted to comfort her, but instead I made it worse. I hadn't known what to say.

I'd asked her name and she said,

'Annabelle.'

She looked up, wiping a cheek with the cuff of her raincoat. Her hood fell back.

'Annabelle,' I said again. 'Your name's Annabelle.'

Her face was bright in the moonlight. I could see her freckles, scattered in their hundreds.

'You don't remember me,' I said. I was breathing so fast I could hardly get the words out. 'It was so long ago. I watched you, I saw you bury your doll. I saw the funeral. And then.'

And then.

And then.

The crying came from nowhere.

That's how it felt.

But that's just a way of saying it was sudden. That it caught me by surprise. It didn't really come from nowhere. Nothing comes from nowhere. It had been inside me for years. I'd never let it out, not really. The truth is I didn't know how. Nobody teaches you that sort of thing. I remember the car journey, when we drove home from Ocean Cove, half a lifetime ago. Mum and Dad were crying to the sound of the radio, but I wasn't crying. I couldn't. And thinking back, I never did.

So here was not crying when I completed Mario 64 in single player mode, with the Player Two control pad tangled, lifeless in the empty space beside me.

And here was not crying the time at the supermarket with Mum, when I let myself forget. I reached to take down the box of strawberry Pop-Tarts from the shelf because Simon liked strawberry Pop Tarts, but nobody else liked strawberry Pop-Tarts, so when I realized what I'd done, I had to put them back. I had to watch myself putting a box of fucking strawberry Pop-Tarts back on a supermarket shelf and hope that Mum didn't see, because if she did it would mean more trips to the doctor, it would be more hours of silence at the kitchen table. Here was not crying at that.

Here were all the other moments when I let myself forget. Each morning of waking up, of believing for the shortest time that everything was normal, everything was okay, before the kick in the guts reminder that nothing was.

Here was every adult conversation that faltered

into silence the second I entered the room. Here was everyone knowing, everyone thinking, everyone trying desperately not to think, that if it wasn't for me, if it wasn't for what I did, he'd still be alive.

Here was every single moment, since I first closed my eyes to count to a hundred, since I opened them to cheat.

It didn't come from nowhere, but it did sort of take me by surprise. The tears falling faster than I could wipe them away. 'I'm so sorry, Simon. I'm so sorry. Forgive me. Please can you forgive me.'

Annabelle could have left me there. I wouldn't have blamed her if she had. I'd frightened her, and now she had her chance to get away. To escape from this madman. But she didn't leave.

'Shhh, shhh. It'll be okay.'

I felt her gently take hold of my hand, heard her whispering to me as I wept.

'You're going to be okay.'

'Forgive me.'

Shhh, shhh.

It'll be okay.

this goodbye, the goodbye

Dr Clement stood to shake hands, clasping my fingers, making it impossible to return a firm grip. 'Matt, good to see you. Richard. Susan. Please, take a seat.'

'Would anyone like a cup of tea?' Claire-or-maybe-Anna offered.

'We're fine,' Mum said in that clipped way of hers, when everyone can tell straight away that she's far from fine. She worried about these meetings more than I did.

She'd arrived on the ward over an hour before, clutching a carrier bag with a neatly folded pair of black trousers, a crisp white shirt and my old school shoes polished to a shine. She ran me a bath in the patients' bathroom, filling it with bubbles. I brushed my teeth, and shaved for the first time in nearly a month. Dad arrived from work a few minutes before the meeting was scheduled to begin. We did our special handshake. He said I looked smart.

'Okay,' said Dr Clement. 'Let's start with introductions.'

There were so many of them. We went around the room, each person saying their name and job title.

I forgot them straight away.

When the student nurse had come to fetch me, he explained there were lots of people; the community team had been invited too, he said. This was a good thing, he explained. They were invited to help with preparations for my discharge from hospital. He offered to sit out if I wanted, except it'd be useful for his learning objectives if he could be involved? I told him his learning objectives were very important to me. I forgot to sound sarcastic. He was grateful, saying I shouldn't worry about there being lots of people, because I was the important one. When the introductions got to me I said, 'Matthew Homes, um, patient.'

Dr Clement studied me for a moment over the rim of his glasses, then let loose a single bark of laughter. 'Good. Well, the purpose of this meeting is to catch up with how things are going for Matthew, and to make some collective decisions about the way we go forwards from here. How are you feeling in yourself, Matt?'

The problem was, because I was the important one, everyone was looking at me. It's hard to think properly with so many different faces staring at you – your thoughts get stuck.

'Actually I will get a cup of tea, if that's okay? My mouth's a bit dry.'

I started to stand up, but Dr Clement gestured for me to stay put, and said he'd make it for me. He said this whilst looking at the student nurse though, which I guess was an invitation for him to offer. He did, and Dr Clement said, 'Thanks Tim, do you mind?'

'No, no. That's fine. How do you take it again Matt?'

'Three sugars please.'

Mum flashed a disapproving look, and I said, 'Or two. It doesn't matter. I can make it myself if—'

'It's okay.' He bounced out of the room.

From the corner, an electric fan licked at the pages of my medical notes. Dad shuffled in his seat, someone else suppressed a yawn, a lady by the window checked her mobile phone, then dropped it into a flowery handbag.

On a low table in the centre of the room sat a box of tissues, a pile of leaflets about different types of mental illness, and a potted plant with sickly-looking leaves. I probably spent too long noticing these things, too long thinking about them. 'Carry on,' Dr Clement said. There was a hint of irritation in his voice. 'In your own words.'

'Shouldn't we wait for, um—'

He tilted his chair onto its back legs, resting his feet on the edge of the table. He wasn't wearing school shoes to make him look presentable. 'It's fine. I'm sure Tim won't mind. Let's make a start. How are you feeling in yourself?'

When I returned from Ocean Cove, they put me on the High Dependency Unit. It was for my own good, they explained. It would help me to feel more settled. In the High Dependency Unit all the doors are locked, the nurses sit in an office behind fortress-thick glass, and we eat with plastic cutlery. My medication was increased, and the nurses would watch me take the tablets, then keep me talking about my mood or my sleep or my weather or my climate, until they could be certain I'd swallowed them. It was around this time that someone first mentioned how it was also available as an injection. Perhaps they were trying to prepare me, but this felt a lot like a threat.

I spent most of my time in bed, or else smoking in the caged square of concrete out the back – always accompanied by a nurse. I had a lot of time to think, and when I wasn't thinking about Simon, who I thought about most, was Annabelle.

'Cup of tea with the sea?'

'What?'

'I was going to have one. You're welcome to join me. I can trust you, can't I?'

The rain wasn't so much falling, as dancing all around in a fine spray, shining silver in the moonlight. I don't know how long I'd been crying, only that I'd stopped. I felt emptied out somehow. I felt strangely calm. Annabelle was still beside me, watching me closely.

She reached into a pocket of her bag, taking out a metal Thermos flask with a small dent near the base. She struggled for a second with the lid before it opened. It let out a squeak as the steam was released into the cold night air. That was strange in itself. Or rather, it wasn't strange enough. I'm a person who reads a lot of meaning into stuff, forever hunting out the small print. You've probably gathered that by now. I don't mean to do it, but I can't help myself. I see symbols. I see tricks of reality. Hidden truths. But there's no small print in a Thermos flask. Not a slightly battered Thermos flask with a lid that is tight enough to make a person struggle, but that eventually opens. Nothing – absolutely nothing – is more ordinary than that.

This was actually happening.

'Or we can go back up to the site if you'd rather? Get some warm soup in you or something? Get you in some dry clothes. You're soaked right through.'

'Um— I—'

'Of course that would mean meeting my dad too. And he'll want to know what you were doing by the caravans. It won't be a big deal, but he will ask. Strictly speaking, you were trespassing you know?'

'I'm sorry, I was— I thought—'

She almost smiled. 'What am I like? You don't have to explain to me. I'm just trying to give you your options, that's all. Because no way can I just leave you here. Not like this. Not to let you—'

She stopped.

I know what she was going to say though. She shook her head inside the hood of her raincoat, 'I'm sorry. That was coming out wrong. I just mean— I'd be worried about you.'

Dr Clement let his chair drop with a decisive thud.

I could feel him mining the small twitches and movements of my face. How was I feeling in myself?

Perhaps I could have told him what it felt like to turn eighteen, incarcerated on a psychiatric ward. I was in the patients' kitchen, watching the kettle boil, trying to hear Simon in the bubbling water. When Mum and Dad appeared in the doorway. Mum was holding a parcel wrapped in gold and silver paper with a silver helium balloon tied around it.

I hadn't even realized what day it was.

'Thanks Mum, thanks Dad.'

We went to my room to unwrap it. The balloon floated up to the ceiling, bouncing its way into a corner.

'If it's not the right one—'

'No. It's good.'

'It was Jacob who recommended it actually,' Dad explained. 'We bumped into him the other day in town, did he tell you?'

'I never see him.'

'He said he was planning to come—'

'I said I never see him, okay!'

I didn't mean to raise my voice like that. It wasn't their fault. 'Sorry. I'm sorry. I didn't mean to shout.'

Dad folded the torn wrapping paper neatly, then looked around for a waste-paper bin before dropping it back on my bed and staring out of the window. Mum was sitting beside me. She stroked my hair behind my ear like she used to when I was little. 'I think he just finds it hard,' she said at last. 'Jacob finds it hard. And we find it hard. It's difficult for the people who love you.'

I stared at my helium balloon hugging the ceiling. 'I'm finding it hard too.'

'I know. Oh, my darling. I know.'

Dad clapped his hands together briskly, in that sudden way he does when he wants to be decisive. When he wants to save us from ourselves. 'Shall we play it then?' he asked.

I pushed the sadness away. I didn't want to be upset when they were trying so hard to make it a nice day. 'It's a really good present,' I said. 'Thank you.'

I meant it too. It wasn't so long ago when I could have wanted nothing more – a PlayStation 3 and some decent games – but now I can't even think which games they were. What I do know is that Mum and Dad were useless at all of them. But that it was sort of fun watching them try. We'd gone down to the TV lounge to plug it in, and took it in turns to play, sitting on the sunken couch or kneeling on the carpet. And not only us, but Thomas and a couple of the other patients joined in too. Euan, I think it was. And maybe Alex. Was it Alex? It doesn't matter, because I've changed all their names anyway. Nobody in this story has their real name. I wouldn't do that to people. Even Claire-or-maybe-Anna is between two other names I can't decide. You don't think I'm really called Matthew Homes, do you? You don't think I'd just give away my whole life to a stranger?

Come on.

It was funny, because whenever it was the person I'm calling Euan's turn to play, he couldn't sit still. He'd move around all over the place, hardly even watching the screen. And he'd make all the noises with his mouth.

'Kerpow! Kerpow!'

He didn't even realize he was doing it.

'Kerpow!'

I thought about when I was younger; a time when I was poorly, genuinely poorly for once, and Mum had helped me to make a den in the living room, and we played Donkey Kong together on my Game Boy Color. 'Do you remember it, Mum?'

She looked at me blankly. Not blankly. But sort of distant – looking right through me to some faraway place. Her voice sounded distant too. 'I don't think I do remember.'

She's never kept much. Not from that time. She doesn't know what she was like – the way she was with me. She doesn't know how her suffering spilled out of her, filling the house. How it controlled her. 'You were fucking mad back then,' I said.

'Kerpow! Kaboom!'

'Sorry, darling?'

But perhaps it's me who has it all muddled up. And anyway – what difference does it really make? She did her best. I guess there's a Use By date when it comes to blaming your parents for how messed up you are.

I guess that's what turning eighteen means.

Time to own it.

'Pardon, darling?' she asked again.

'Nothing. It's not important.'

I leaned into her, letting my head rest gently against her shoulder. I listened to her breathing. When it was my turn to play, I let Thomas take another turn instead. I nestled into the nook of Mum's arm. Then lay on a cushion on her lap. I fell asleep like that. She's all bones and hard edges. She's never been comfortable, but she's always been there.

'Ka Blamo!'

That evening they both stayed on the ward for supper. Usually supper was just sandwiches, but to celebrate my birthday Dad bought fish and chips for the entire ward – all the staff and patients. The dining room rustled with chip paper. The whole building smelled of salt and vinegar.

Mum disappeared partway through, then the lights went out, and she came back in with a chocolate birthday cake and eighteen flickering candles. Everyone broke out in a loud chorus of Happy Birthday. Simon joined in too.

He was in the flames.

Of course he was in the flames.

A nurse grabbed hold of my wrist, leading me quickly to the clinic where she held my blistering fingers under the cold tap. I had no idea what I'd done, only that I had been trying to hold him.

My medication was changed yet again. More side effects. More sedation. In time, Simon grew more distant. I looked in the rain clouds, fallen leaves, sideways glances. I searched for him in the places I had come to expect him. In running tap water. In spilled salt. I listened in the spaces between words.

At first I wondered if he was angry with me, if he'd given up? It made me feel sad to think like that. I don't know which one of us was most dependent on the other. Over the next few weeks, I would lie in my bed, listening to fragments of conversation drifting from the nurses' office, to the scraping of the viewing slats. And I would watch my helium balloon slowly die.

The worst thing about this illness isn't the things it makes me believe, or what it makes me do. It's not the control that it has over me, or even the control it's allowed other people to take.

Worse than all of that is how I have become selfish.

Mental illness turns people inwards. That's what I reckon. It keeps us forever trapped by the pain of our own minds, in the same way that the pain of a broken leg or a cut thumb will grab your attention, holding it so tightly that your good leg or your good thumb seem to cease to exist.

I'm stuck looking inwards. Nearly every thought I have is about me – this whole story has been all about me; the way I felt, what I thought, how I grieved. Perhaps that's the kind of thing Dr Clement wanted to hear about?

But what I said was, 'I haven't done anything wrong.'

'Sure. Sure. But people have been worried about you. Why is that, do you think?'

'I don't—'

The doctor nearest me lifted my file of medical notes, but Dr Clement said, 'It's fine, Nicola. We don't need to write anything. Let's just listen to Matthew.'

She put her pen down, her face flushing pink. The doctors have a hierarchy, and Dr Clement is at the very top. He's my consultant psychiatrist. What he says, goes.

'I want to go home,' I said.

'Where's home?' Annabelle asked.

She had asked me to walk down to the cove with her. I didn't protest. There was something in the way she looked at me – a look somewhere between determined and pleading. And maybe I felt that I owed her something.

The rain had stopped. The air was still. Pebbles crunched

beneath our feet as we reached the shoreline, where small dark waves broke into frothy white.

'I live in Bristol,' I told her. 'I've got my own flat. I mean— I don't own it or anything.'

The sea looked like black silk. Or maybe velvet. I always confuse those two. It looked nice is what I'm getting at. It was the same black as the sky, so looking out to the horizon you couldn't be sure where the sea stopped and the sky started.

And the moon was huge. And everywhere, the stars were scattered in their millions.

'It must be nice living here,' I said.

'I live in a bloody caravan, Matt. With my dad. It's not nice living here.'

'You haven't seen my flat.'

She laughed at that. I wasn't trying to be funny, but it felt nice seeing her laugh. She laughed a lot. She's a person who might say, 'Well if you don't laugh, you'll cry.'

She didn't actually say that, but I can easily imagine it. She seemed nice. I reckon anyone who would stay to comfort a stranger whilst they wept their life out must be fairly nice. It was more than that though. She had a way about her too. Like everything was important, but nothing was so important that it couldn't be interrupted with another offer of tea from her flask, or a question about if you were warm enough because it would be really no trouble at all to go back to the site, to borrow you one of her dad's jumpers. And she's sorry that you're having a hard time, she really is. But it'll all be okay. She's certain of it.

She's known sadness. That's what it is. I only just thought that as I wrote it. She's known sadness, and it has made her kind.

'She didn't have a name,' she said.

We had walked along the shore, and then back on ourselves towards the scattering of beach huts. And now we were sitting side by side on a small upturned wooden rowing boat. Our knees were almost touching.

'She wasn't my favourite doll. If she did have a name it would have changed every time I played with her. But when you saw us. When you watched her funeral. She was called Mummy.'

She knew that. Because they all were.

If I'd counted to a hundred the day before then I might have watched her bury a Barbie in the dirt, or the day before that a Furby, or a rabbit from the Sylvanian Families. And all of them were called Mummy.

'Jesus,' Annabelle said. She put her face in her hands even though it was too dark to properly see her blushing. 'What was I like?'

The only difference with the funeral I saw, was what she kept.

'The coat?'

'It's meant to be a dress.'

She took the piece of yellow cloth from her pocket, but she didn't hand it to me. It's strange. She trusted me enough to be alone with me in the night-time. But there was something about the way she held it, her small fist closed tightly. I knew this wasn't an invitation to take it again. 'We made it together,' she said. 'It was supposed to be a dress, but Mum let me help a bit too much and it ended up— It is more like a coat, you're right.'

It became a comforter. Her friends teased her because she was never without it. That's what she told me. It's worn right through in places from where she rubs it between her thumb and fingers whenever she's watching TV or reading. And it's grubby too. More brown than yellow really. It even smells a bit. She laughed loudly as she said that, as she told me she's never once put it in the washing machine in case it falls apart.

And all of this somehow made it more real. Like it couldn't possibly be Simon's comfort blanket because it had its own story. Because it was Annabelle's.

'I would never have kept it all this time,' she said. Suddenly serious, suddenly looking straight at me. 'I don't suppose I would have done. Except it took on more meaning after what happened. And in a way, I suppose that's because of you.'

Dr Clement glanced to my dad with an apologetic wince. Dad nodded slowly. 'Let's do this another way,' Dr Clement continued. 'I'd like to ask you the difficult question.'

Instinctively I found myself reaching for Mum's hand. Not because I needed comfort, but perhaps to offer her some. This is my care plan: As a small boy I killed my own brother, and now I must kill him again. I'm given medicine to poison him, then questioned to make sure he's dead.

Dr Clement lowered his voice. 'Tell me,' he said. 'Is Simon in the room with us? Is your brother still talking to you?'

The door swung open, the student nurse bounced in, spilling

tea on his hand, 'Ouch! Here you go, Matt. Sorry it took so long.'

'Thanks.'

'We were out of sugar. I had to get some from the store cupboard—'

'It's fine, Tim,' Claire-or-maybe-Anna said softly, gesturing him to sit.

Then the whole room was looking at me again. I must have answered too quietly because Dr Clement said he was terribly sorry, but could I speak up a little.

Someone pressed the button on the electric fan, bringing the whirring blades to a halt.

She didn't mean what had happened between us.

The way I'd pushed her over in the dirt as she had her toy funeral. As she tried to make this goodbye, the goodbye; the one she thought she needed.

No. She wasn't talking about that, because she didn't remember it. She has no recollection of a small boy spying on her, or how she had shouted at me, and told me that I'd ruined everything.

And if that's hard to believe then maybe think back through your own life, to when you were eight or nine years old. See if the memories you have are the ones you might expect. Or if they are fragments, dislocated moments, a smell here, a feeling there. The unlikeliest conversations and places. We don't choose what we keep – not at that age. Not ever, really.

So she hasn't kept that. But she has kept some memories around it. This is how we piece together our past. We do it like a jigsaw puzzle, where there are missing pieces. But so long as we have enough of the pieces, we can know what belongs in the gaps.

A piece that Annabelle has, is of her doll coming back from the grave.

'It was a few weeks after—'

Annabelle stopped to interrupt herself. She said it was cold. She said I was soaked to the skin, would I not rather go and get some dry clothes?

'I'm okay here,' I said. 'I'm not cold. Are you?'

'No. I'm fine,' she said. 'It's hard to talk about. I don't want to upset you. We could talk about something else? Perhaps you'd rather be getting home?'

I hadn't told her that home was currently a mental hospital. But I would. Before this evening was over. Before finding myself on a twilight bus with an extra jumper, with an apple and a Snickers bar and a cheese sandwich. Before that, I'd tell her everything.

'It was a few weeks after the accident, the horrible accident. With your—'

Simon wasn't saying anything. He was listening though. He was on the shoreline. He was in the shallowest ripples. He was making pebbles shiny.

'Is that what it was?' I asked.

'What do you mean?'

'Is that what people called it? An accident?'

'Of course. Of course that's what it was. You blame yourself, don't you?'

'Sometimes. A lot, recently.'

She shook her head, 'My dad blamed himself too. For not putting a rail up even though he'd been meaning to. For not putting a sign up. For being too sad to do much at all. But it wasn't his fault either.'

And that's what the policeman had come to say when he brought Annabelle's doll back in a brown paper bag. The policeman – the policeman with a bushy ginger-brown moustache and glasses. The same policeman who had taken a statement from me. He was an old family friend. More a friend of Annabelle's mummy, really. They'd gone to college together. He'd gone to the wedding. He'd gone to her funeral. He knew how much Annabelle's dad was struggling – drinking too much, taking too much on. He was looking for excuses to check up on him from time to time. He needed excuses, because Annabelle's dad is the kind of man who would never ask for help.

He's like me.

So when a brief investigation into the death of Simon Homes reached the verdict of a tragic accident – this family friend looked for an excuse, and he found one in the small cloth doll that was discovered at the scene. That I had carefully placed under my brother's head, to make him comfortable.

It was a poor judgement, perhaps. No. Definitely.

The policeman didn't stop to think that Annabelle may run in to say hello. He didn't stop to think that she had no bedtime any more. No bath time. No story time. He didn't really think at all. But sometimes all the stars in the entire universe conspire to make something good happen.

'I just froze,' Annabelle said.

And she was sort of reliving it as she told me. She was staring ahead at the big black sea, but in the place in her head where pictures form she was standing in the small reception area. Her dad and Uncle Mike the Policeman were talking. A stilted, awkward conversation. And there on the counter, an arm flopped awkwardly, face tilted, staring back at her, was her dead dolly.

'Jesus,' she said. 'What did he think my dad was going to do? Give her a wash, bring her through to me. Here you go Bella-Boo, here's your dolly back. Uncle Mike thought you might want it. By the way. It was found under the dead little boy! Fuck! Shit! I'm sorry. I'm so sorry, Matt.'

'It's okay,' I said.

And I meant it too.

Dr Clement offered a small glance to the other doctor, then they turned back to me.

'No, he isn't,' I said. 'Simon isn't speaking to me. He isn't here. He isn't in the room. He died a long time ago.'

Mum snatched a tissue from the table.

Dr Clement cleared his throat. 'My feeling is that you've been making real progress—'

'Can I go home?'

'As I say, you're making progress but these things take a while. It's best not to rush. We'll try some short periods of leave first, away from the ward. One evening at a time. It's early days for you to be at your flat by yourself but—'

'He can stay with us,' Mum said. 'He can stay with us. We can look after him.'

'That's an option, certainly.'

I can't remember too much after that. It was difficult to keep up. So I don't know exactly when the lady from the community team started talking. She was looking forward to working with me, but this wasn't about who would look after me, it was about laying a path for me to look after myself.

That's how she put it, anyway.

I never know how to respond when people say stuff like that, how to fill the expectant silence that always comes attached.

'What's your name again?'

She smiled, 'It's Denise. Denise Lovell. Good to meet you.'

I stared at the sickly plant for a while, and eventually Dr Clement made a show of looking at his watch, saying how productive this had all been.

It was sort of awkward because he cut straight over a man who was still enthusiastically talking about some Day Centre, where there were lots of groups that I'd be more than welcome to attend.

'Sorry, Steve.' Dr Clement said. 'I'm just aware of the time.'

'No, no. I was wrapping up. Just to say that the Art Group's very popular. I hear you're good at Art, Matt? Oh, and we'll be getting a computer at long last, so there's that too.'

He nodded at me. And winked.

The policeman left, taking the doll away with him, making a silent gesture to Annabelle's father, with his fingers held to his face like a telephone receiver, mouthing the words, 'I'll call you tomorrow, mate.'

Annabelle felt her toes lifting from the floor.

She landed with a gentle bump on her daddy's lap. If she closes her eyes and concentrates, she can still feel the warmth of his hand against her teary cheek, the way he held her face to his chest. She can still feel the edge of his tie tickling against the side of her nose. She can still hear their conversation.

They didn't talk about the dolls. They didn't talk about the little boy. What they talked about, properly talked about – and for the first time since she had died three months before – was her mummy.

Annabelle told her dad about the way her mummy had said sorry to her over and over again when she explained about the cancer. How she said sorry like it was her own fault somehow, but that it wasn't her own fault was it? And Annabelle's daddy explained that this was because she didn't want to not be there for her, to not be there for Annabelle to turn to whenever life got difficult. Because life can be difficult. But that she could always come to him, always, and that they could always think about what Mummy would say.

'Mummy would want you to keep reading me bedtime stories,' Annabelle said.

'She would, wouldn't she?'

'Yes.'

'And she'd want me to make you eat your vegetables, all of them. Even the broccoli.'

'No.'

'Wouldn't she?'

Annabelle pressed her face into his shirt and said a muffled, 'Yes. She would want that. But she would want you to stay and watch me at ballet lessons and not go to the pub until I finish.'

If she closes her eyes and concentrates, Annabelle can still hear it all.

'I think you're right. I think you're right.'

She remembers holding the little yellow doll's dress to her chin, stroking it between her finger and thumb as they talked.

The funeral had been too big and strange. And everything since had been empty. But sitting on her dad's knee, sitting long into the night because they both agreed that this one time, just this once, her mummy wouldn't give her a bedtime – they began to say goodbye.

'It was a memorial,' Annabelle said to me.

She was smiling now. She had cried a bit and her eyes were wet and sparkly. But she was smiling as she said, 'It was the beginning of things getting better.'

I stood up from the upturned boat and felt the pebbles shift beneath my boots.

'Are you okay?' Annabelle asked.

'What was that word you said?'

'When?'

'What you called it. A memorial, was it?'

'That's what it felt like.'

'It sounded nice.'

'It was. It really was.'

'Annabelle. I'm ready to go now.'

The sun doesn't set in the east. But seeing the light blue band stretching across the horizon, it looked just about ready to rise.

After the meeting, Mum and Dad took me to the hospital canteen. We ordered two coffees and a hot chocolate with squirty cream and a flake. 'I can stay with you then?' I asked.

'You always can,' Mum said.

'I mean, on leave or whatever. Away from this place?'

'That's what Dr Clement said.'

'That's a bit of good news, isn't it?'

'Yes. It is.'

We went quiet then, sipping at our drinks. A lady with a hairnet came around wiping tables. Someone in the queue for the tills dropped their tray, then stared at the mess as if willing it to tidy itself. An announcement came over the loudspeaker saying something about something else. People came and went. We didn't talk for ages. Then I said, 'I want to do something.'

'Uh-huh?'

'Not now. Next summer.'

'Well that's a way away,' Dad said.

'I know. But I'm too— I'm too ill at the moment. I need to get better first. I know that now.'

Mum put down her cup. 'Well what is it?'

'I don't want to say. But you have to tell me I can. You have to tell me that I'm allowed.'

'Well—'

'No. I need you to trust me.'

Dad leaned in and spoke quietly. 'Ami. It isn't that we don't trust you, but we can't just agree to—'

It was strange that it happened this way around. I would never have guessed it would be my mum lifting her fingers to her mouth, stopping my dad from asking.

'We trust you,' she said. 'It's fine. Whatever you need to do. We trust you.'

keepsake

I wrote the invitation letters sitting right here.

They were the first things I wrote on this computer, before I even thought to write my story on it. I still have them saved, but I needed Steve's help finding them again. He was a bit distracted. They all are today. You have to hand it to them though – keeping the doors open right to the end.

'Steve.'

They've even had the kitchen open, and the occupational therapist has been in there with some of the others, making a Goodbye Everybody cake.

'Steve. You busy?'

He was taking down notices from the pinboard. 'Hey Matt. Sorry. I was a million miles away. How ya doin'?'

'I'm okay. How are you?'

'Ah, you know. Bit hectic. Lots of boxes.'

'If you're too busy?'

'No, no. What's up?'

I told him what I was after, and he pulled up a chair to sit beside me. He did that thing where you spin the chair around and sit on it back to front, with his arms folded casually on the backrest. 'Some time last summer was it?'

'Yeah. But don't worry if you can't—'

'We can but try, eh?'

Whilst he clicked through the folders and files, he mentioned something about there being public computers in the library too. 'It might be worth— if you're not already a member, that is. It might be worth joining up,' he suggested. 'So you can carry on with—'

All my printouts, all my typewriter pages – the whole lot is stacked in an untidy pile beside the keyboard. It was Jeanette from Art Group who added my drawings. When I arrived this morning she was quietly clearing up the art room, taking down posters, putting brushes into boxes. But then she stopped clearing things away and moved to the big table, where all the paintings and pictures that have been left behind were carefully laid out.

I stood in the doorway watching as Jeanette gently stroked her thumb over one of Patricia's poster paint rainbows. I didn't want to interrupt, but she caught sight of me and smiled. 'Aren't they all wonderful? Yours too, Matt. They're wonderful. You must take them home and keep them safe.'

It's the first time I've put it all together. All the words and pictures. Steve gestured to the pile, stopping just short of patting it like a little dog.

'I won't need to use the library computers,' I told him. 'I'm finishing it today.'

That even surprised me, how sure I sounded. But I am sure. I have a whole hour stretched out in front of me, and I'm getting pretty fast at typing. The lady at the front desk says I'm quicker than her now. I'm not, but I reckon I'm probably getting close. And anyway, it was kind of her to say it.

'Ah. Here we are,' Steve said. 'July the eighteenth. Does that sound about right?'

'They're letters.'

He double-clicked, and they all popped up on the screen. That sort of nudged me back a bit. I felt my grip giving way, felt myself slipping down the thread of time.

'Is this what you're after?' Steve asked.

Patricia walked behind us, wearing her leopard-skin leotard top and a pair of Lycra leggings. She was carrying a bowl of crisps in one hand, and a bowl of peanuts in the other. Someone else was behind her with a plate of sausage rolls.

I guess that nudged me back a bit too.

'Is this what you're after, Matt?' Steve asked again.

'Yeah. That's it. Thanks Steve.'

18th July 09

Dear Aunty Mel,

I hope that you are well and enjoying the summer. I hope that
Uncle Brian is well too, and Peter and Sam. This letter is for all
of you. I'll be writing a separate one to Aaron in London.

Thank you for the cards you sent me when I was in hospital.
I know it's a long time to wait to say thank you and I'm sorry for
that. I'll get to the point. Did you know that it is nearly 10 years
exactly since Simon died? His accident happened on August
15th 1999. I have decided that on August 15th this year it would
be good to have a memorial.

I have done the arranging myself. The memorial will be in
Bristol at the Beavers and Brownies Hut near to Mum and Dad.
I did think of having it at the church hall but Simon found
church dead boring. And if you remember we had his tenth
birthday at the Beavers and Brownies Hut and that was
really good.

The memorial will be at 12 o'clock. I hope you can come.

Love Matt.

18th July 09

Dear Aaron and Jenny,

I hope that you are well and enjoying the summer. Nanny Noo
tells me that the summer feels hotter in London because of all
the traffic. It's hot here too.

It's Matt by the way. Aaron's cousin. I know it's not like me to
write so I will start by thanking you for the Christmas cards you
always send me. I'm crap at that sort of thing.

Aaron did you know it is nearly ten years to the day that Simon
died? There will be a memorial for him which I am arranging at
the Beavers and Brownies Hut near to my parents' house at 12
o'clock on August 15th. I know that you are very busy with your
new job at the bank but it is a Saturday so I hope you will be able
to come. You can stay at my flat if you need somewhere to stay.

See you then hopefully, Matt.

P.S. Jenny. I know you never met Simon but he would have really
liked you so please come too if you want. Also I'm really sorry if
I've got your name wrong. Part of me thinks it's Gemma. Please
forgive me if I got it wrong. Not making excuses, but I am a
schizophrenic.

18th July 09

Dear Aunt Jacqueline,

It's Matthew Homes. Your nephew. It's been a long time since I
saw you and I know that is because you don't really get on that
well with my mum. Nor do I some of the time, so I understand.

I would like to invite you to a 10 year memorial for my brother
Simon. It will be at the Brownies and Beavers Hut near to Mum
and Dad's house on August 15th at 12 o'clock. I've already
hired it.

I hope to see you then. Also I know you smoke quite a lot and so
do I. So we can keep each other company.

Matt

18th July 09

Dear Nanny Noo and Granddad,

Nanny I really wanted to tell you about this when you came
to see me on Thursday but I knew you would want to get an
invitation in the post like everyone else.

Guess what I have done? Last week I looked up the number for
the Brownies Hut near to Mum and Dad's, and I have booked it
for August 15th.

I have decided to arrange a memorial. I didn't really know
what they were, but do you remember what I told you about
Annabelle? How she sort of had one for her mum? That got me
thinking. It got me thinking a lot. And I think we should do one
too. I've been planning it for ages. You don't have to, but if you
want to help me make the sandwiches and stuff then you can.
But you really don't have to. See you next Thursday. See you
soon Granddad – I hope your cough is getting better.

Love Matt

July 18th 09

Dear Mum and Dad,

Last year when I was in hospital I told you that I wanted to do something this summer. I didn't tell you what it was but you said that you trusted me to do it anyway.

I never said thank you. So thank you.

On 15th August we are having a memorial for Simon. I have invited the whole family. Or I will invite them but I need you to tell me their addresses first. I've written the invitation letters already and I've bought all the envelopes and stamps. I've also booked the Brownies and Beavers Hut for 12 o'clock. I will bring all the food.

I hope you will understand that I had to do this by myself. I needed it to be something that I did for him, because you already did so much – but I never got to.

Love Matthew

Knock

Knockknock

Of course, of course she came to help.

'You didn't have to bring stuff, Nanny.'

'Nonsense. It's just a few bits and bobs. It's not right you buying everything.'

I was so pleased to see her. I hadn't slept well. I know it wasn't much to arrange, but when the day arrived I was full of worries. Nanny stepped into my kitchen and saw the tower of hurriedly cut ham sandwiches, stacked on the counter. 'Wonderful,' she said. 'You're nearly done. Now you remembered Aunt Jacky's vegetarian?'

'Is she?'

Nanny smiled and budged me aside with a swing of her hip. 'You've done lots. Let me take over for a while. You get washed and dressed.'

By the time I was out of the shower, all the sandwiches were in neat triangles on a serving tray, and she was crouched in front of the oven checking on the mini sausage rolls. 'Good timing,' she said. 'Help me up. My knees are on their way out, I'm sure of it. I'll be as bad as your granddad soon.'

I helped her to her feet. 'I've bought crisps too,' I said. 'Should I put them in bowls?'

'We can do that when we're there, sweetheart. They'll stay fresher in the packs.'

'Yeah. Sorry. I'm a bit— I want it to be perfect.'

Nanny Noo didn't respond to that straight away. She lit a

menthol cigarette from her secret pack in my kitchen drawer, blowing the smoke out of the window. She only smoked half before stubbing it out. Then she placed her hand against my cheek, and kissed me on my forehead. 'It doesn't need to be perfect,' she said at last. 'It's already wonderful.'

'Thank you, Nanny.'

She tapped on the kitchen counter, 'Now, you start taking some of this down to the car. I can't go up and down those stairs. Not with these knees.'

'Thank you.'

It wasn't perfect.

There were things I didn't properly think through. Take the Beavers and Brownies Hut. It's bigger than I remembered, and there weren't really that many of us.

When the man met Nanny and me in the car park to give us the keys – and to explain how important it was not to prop open the fire doors with anything, because they'd had trouble with that before, and the amateur dramatics troop were unlikely to be allowed to rehearse there next summer if they didn't stop scuffing the floor with black-soled footwear, and how to open and shut the top windows with the hook on the pole, and a bunch of other stuff that I didn't properly listen to – he asked how many were in our group, then looked at me like I'd made a mistake.

Aaron and Jenny couldn't make it. They sent a message with Aunty Mel to say they were so sorry but it was a friend's wedding and Aaron was Best Man. There was nothing they could do, but their thoughts were with us, and they hoped to see everyone soon.

Aunty Mel did come, and she brought my youngest cousin, Sam. But Uncle Brian had to work, and Peter was away on some trekking weekend with the Duke of Edinburgh's Awards.

'If he didn't go,' Aunty Mel explained in a whisper. 'He'd miss out on his silver.'

'Of course, of course,' Mum whispered back. 'Well, he's got lovely weather for it hasn't he? If it's anything like here. Almost too hot for hiking, I'd think.'

'Beautiful, isn't it? The forecast says it might turn tomorrow though.'

We were all hovering at the long fold-out table, where Nanny Noo had helped me to lay out the food and bottles of fizzy pop. Behind us was a small circle of chairs that I'd set out, and behind them were about fifty more, all stacked up against the far wall.

'I didn't ask about your drive, Mel?' Dad said. Except he probably did ask, because she went to their house first to freshen up. And knowing my dad, it was the first thing he asked.

'Oh it wasn't too bad, thanks Richard.' Aunty Mel turned to Sam, 'Was it darling?'

Sam shrugged, stuffing a sausage roll in his mouth and Aunty Mel continued, 'Although there was a bit of traffic build-up coming onto—'

'The M4,' Dad interrupted, nodding vigorously. 'That's right. I did ask, because you said you didn't have time to stop at the services.'

'Oh, yes. Yes. Still. Just as well. They're extortionate these days, aren't they? I read somewhere recently they were going to introduce some new laws to curb that.'

'But it's a captive market, isn't it?' Dad said. 'It's ridiculous. Five pounds for a cheese toastie.'

'And the rest,' Mum said.

'And the rest,' Dad said.

———

'Are you joining us for cake, Matt?'

That was the student social worker – the one with the gold hooped earrings. She just took a sneaky peek over my shoulder as she skipped by.

It'll be all awkward conversations there too. 'Um— I'll be through in a bit,' I told her. 'I'm nearly done.'

'No rush,' she said.

It's hard to concentrate today, with so much going on.

———

Nobody cared about the prices at motorway service stations. Nobody wanted to be having this conversation.

It was just hard to know how to begin, because we're not one of those families like you get in EastEnders, where all they ever talk about is the big and important stuff. We're the kind of family who don't talk very much at all, and when we do talk, it isn't really about anything.

The conversation trailed off, and all you could hear was the clicking of the wall clock, until Mum asked Jacqueline, 'Any nice plans for the rest of summer?'

When I last saw Aunt Jacqueline she would always dress in black and even wear black lipstick. And she always had a cigarette hanging from her lips. But now she wore a brightly coloured flowing dress and a pink headscarf, and she didn't smoke at all.

'Pardon?' she asked.

Mum had taken a bite of sandwich and had to chew for ages before she could swallow it, 'Sorry. Any nice plans for the rest of summer?'

'We might go away again,' Aunt Jacqueline answered breezily, linking arms with her new boyfriend, who was staring at the bowls of crisps.

'Oh lovely,' Mum said.

'But we haven't decided yet, have we?'

'Hmm? No, no.'

Aunt Jacqueline's new boyfriend was really tall and thin, and wore cut-off denim shorts and sandals. He had long white hair in a ponytail, and a scruffy white beard. He was a vegan.

Nanny Noo could have kicked herself because it was her who insisted we used proper butter in the sandwiches, instead of my tub of margarine. So all he could eat were the crisps. Except even that was a problem because Aunt Jacqueline's new boyfriend wouldn't eat the Beef & Onion flavoured crisps, and instead of just not eating them he gave this sort of hushed lecture about how he had a moral uneasiness with foods that were flavoured to taste like animals, even if they didn't have animals in them.

Mum looked at me, and rolled her eyes.

'Is there a toilet?' asked Sam.

'Just through there,' Nanny Noo pointed.

Then we all took our seats, with our paper plates on our knees, and listened to the sound of Sam's loud trickle of piss through the thin toilet door.

So it wasn't perfect. But that didn't matter. Because this wasn't about what was in the sandwiches, or the huge empty space around our little huddle of chairs. Maybe it took us a while, but then Nanny Noo was right all along. It was wonderful.

'Good lad, weren't he?'

Granddad loosened his tie and undid his top button. He was wearing his smart white shirt, but you could see the dirt still under his fingernails from an early start on the allotment. I think it took courage for him to speak first. He keeps himself to himself, which is why you haven't got to know him too well. But one thing I've learnt about people, is that they can always surprise you.

My granddad wasn't finished, 'Brightened up the room, he did. Just by being there.'

I'm not reading into it. I'm trying not to read into it. But if I did, I doubt I'd be alone. At that exact moment bright sunlight came pouring through the top windows. We had the fire door propped open to let the air in, and with the sunshine came the gentlest breeze, so that all at once it felt warm and cool, and everywhere around us, tiny golden dust particles were swirling in their millions.

There was a collective intake of breath. Nanny Noo squeezed Aunty Mel's hand. Aunt Jacqueline moved her fingers slowly through the air. Mum was welling up already.

It was all lost on Granddad. 'No bloody patience, mind. Would he wait for the glue to dry before he started painting that plane? Remember it? The Sopwith Camel? Not a chance.'

'Was I there?' Sam asked suddenly. He'd been looking a bit bored until then, slouched back and picking at a spot on his neck. Now he sat forwards, scraping his chair legs over the polished wooden floor. 'I think I was there,' he said. 'And Peter and Aaron. I remember you building Airfix with us. Is the Sopwith the one with two sets of wings?'

'It's called a biplane,' Granddad said.

'Yeah. Yeah! Simon wanted to paint mine too. He wanted to paint a face on it. I remember it. Shit. That was so long ago.'

'Language,' Aunty Mel said curtly. 'Honestly. This boy of mine.' She wasn't really cross with him. She reached to ruffle his hair, and you could tell she wasn't really cross.

Then Mum turned to Granddad, and with a smile so big it nudged a tear from her eye, she said, 'Dad. Remember at the lakes? When only you were allowed to help him on the potty.'

Nanny Noo shook her head, 'Oh that was funny, that was so funny.'

Then Mum did something I'd never seen her do before. She did an impression of Simon. 'I want Granddad to wipe my bum, Mummy! Not you. Granddad!'

My granddad threw his head back, laughing so hard you could

see his gold teeth at the back of his mouth. 'I was lucky that trip, weren't I?'

The Beavers and Brownies Hut didn't feel so big after that – the memories could hardly fit. We went on holidays, and to the school nativity when Simon was the Inn Keeper and decided that there was a room for Mary and Joseph after all. We went to the Bristol Exploratory, where we froze our shadows against the glow-in-the-dark wallpaper. We climbed up to the dangerous tree house with a rusty nail, and then off for the tetanus injection that followed. We stood in the queue for the Ghost Train, three times over, always too scared by the time we reached the front. We scrunched through autumn leaves at the arboretum – the trip when Simon disappeared for a whole hour, and Mum was frantic, but Simon didn't even know he was lost, and when we found him, he was happily teaching a bemused elderly couple how to tell the time, but he might need some help from them, but not until he asked.

The truth is, I didn't say that much myself. I didn't have so many memories of my own to share. Not whole memories, with beginnings, middles, and ends. I was only a little boy when I knew my big brother, and we don't get to choose what we keep.

What I did at the memorial, was listen.

To the laughter and the tears, and to the quiet stillness that followed.

This is where I want to leave my story, because it's the place I am most proud of.

But that doesn't make it the end.

This story doesn't have an end. Not really. How can it when I'm still here, still living it? When I print out these last pages I'll turn the computer off, and later today men will come with boxes to take everything away. The lights of Hope Road Day Centre will be switched off for the last time. But in time, another day centre will open and close, and another, and there will always be a Nurse This and a Nurse That, a *Click-Click-Wink* and a Claire-or-maybe-Anna.

I've told you about my first stretch in hospital, but I've been back in since. And I know I will again. We move in circles, this illness and me. We are electrons orbiting a nucleus.

The plan is always the same: After I'm discharged, I spend a couple of weeks with my parents to help me to settle. Mum wishes I was nine again; we could build a den in the living room, and hide away forever. Dad takes it seriously. He holds back on the special handshakes and talks to me like I'm a man. They're both helpful in their own way. The first few days are hardest. The silence is a problem. I get used to the hourly checks, the scraping of viewing slats, fragments of conversations drifting from the nurses' office. I get used to having Simon around. It takes time to adjust, and time to adjust when he's gone.

I could keep on going, but you know what I'm like. The ink running dry from my typewriter ribbon. This place shutting down. That's enough small print to get anyone thinking.

So I'll stack these pages with the rest of them, and leave it all behind. Writing about the past is a way of reliving it, a way of seeing it unfold all over again. We place memories on pieces of paper to know they will always exist. But this story has never been a keepsake – it's finding a way to let go. I don't know the ending, but I know what happens next. I walk along the corridor towards the sound of a Goodbye Party. But I won't get that far. I'll take a left, then a right, and I will push open the front door with both hands.

I have nothing else to do today.

It's a beginning.

Acknowledgements

I would like to thank my parents and sister, who I know will be so proud to see this book on the shelves. I am blessed to have such a supportive family.

I'm grateful to everyone who has read my writing and shared their thoughts. That is no small offering. It is - I've learnt - how a novel comes to exist. Thank you Kev Hawkins and Hazel Ryder, who read my earliest drafts, and whose words of encouragement remained with me. Tanya Atapattu, for so many reasons - but especially for your kind encouragement whenever it was most needed. And Phil Bambridge for your generous contribution to the science lesson in the Prodrome chapter.

A very special thank you to Emma Anderson for your incisive editorial notes, and unfailingly helpful advice.

I completed the first draft of this novel on the Creative Writing MA at Bath Spa University. Thank you again to my parents, who helped support me financially during this time, and also to my then flatmate, Samantha Barron, who endured every vicissitude of my studies with me. Thank you to my manuscript tutor, Tricia Wastvedt, and to my other tutors and fellow students, not least Samantha Harvey, Gerard Woodward, John Jennings, and Nick Stott.

ACKNOWLEDGEMENTS

Thank you to Ellie Gee, for helping me explore Matthew's sketches. And to the artist, Charlotte Farmer, who has brought them to life in these pages.

I am hugely indebted to my literary agent Sophie Lambert of Tibor Jones & Associates, whose guidance – both on and off the page – was invaluable; to my editor, Louisa Joyner, and the wonderful team at HarperFiction, who turned my hopes of a book into a book; and to Nichole Argyres and the team at SMP, who with such care helped to shape this US edition.

Lastly, mostly, Emily Parker. For all of the endless reasons, this novel is dedicated to you.

THE SHOCK OF
THE FALL
by Nathan Filer

About the Author
- A Conversation with Nathan Filer

Behind the Novel
- A Bonus, Never-Before-Published Chapter!

Keep on Reading
- Recommended Reading
- Reading Group Questions

A
Reading
Group Gold
Selection

For more reading group suggestions
visit www.readinggroupgold.com.

 ST. MARTIN'S GRIFFIN

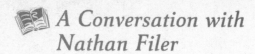
A Conversation with Nathan Filer

What inspired you to write *The Shock of the Fall*?

It's funny—only published authors get asked what inspired them. If you had peered into my bedroom/office/entire world three years ago, I reckon you'd have gone with *possessed*.

This was such a challenging story to write—a search in the dark, when often I wasn't even sure what I was looking for. Then, on page 248, Mum and Dad cough in their sleep and '...we both froze. Simon made a show of it, making his whole body rigid, only his eyes moving from side to side, grinning at me.' And I think: That's it. That's real.

It's not a sentence anyone will stop to re-read, or copy out into their notebook. But it was the right sentence. I got to see him there.

I'm inspired by those moments, by the process.

Of course I also got to spend time in the company of Matthew Homes, who I grew to like enormously. Perhaps compelled is the right word. I felt *compelled* to tell his story.

What was it like to inhabit Matthew's character when writing *The Shock of the Fall*, especially when he is experiencing such mental turmoil?

I never had the experience we sometimes hear writers talk about, when a character arrives in their imagination fully formed. I had a reasonable sense of Matt, but he's a complicated young man. So I got to know him by spending time in his company.

We'd pace the paving slabs in my back garden, with a mug of cold tea and a roll-up, muttering a few dozen versions of the same paragraph; stripping back anything too sentimental, too indulgent or too me.

"It's strange now letting him go."

I was holding down a job whilst writing, so I often wrote very late at night or in the small hours of the morning, when all edges seem blurred, not least our own. At times like that I wasn't really sure who was inhabiting who.

Certainly I felt his emotional journey (and at times his sleep deprivation) but I also know that I'm lucky. Mental health is such a fragile thing, and—comparatively, at least—mine is robust. Matt was always having a harder time than me. My task was to be sensitive towards him, to prioritize his priorities—and to be kind. It's strange now letting him go. I feel protective, somehow. But I'm also very proud to be able to share his story. We'll inhabit each other for a good while yet.

There is an incredible build-up in the reader's realization of what has happened to Matthew and to Simon, how did you create that suspense?

Ah, thank you. It was a challenge writing suspense into the novel, especially since I decided that the main 'event' of the story would be signposted so early on. But of course this is a trick of suspense: give some, hold some back. I was always aiming for a page-turner and that demands an underlying suspense to be maintained throughout. I took this task seriously, enrolling on a Creative Writing MA and taking a module in Suspense Fiction.

Did you read whilst writing *The Shock of the Fall*? If so, what?

Iain Banks' Frank Cauldhame, Mark Haddon's Christopher Boone and Salinger's Holden Caulfield were among the characters who I met whilst still grappling with the tricky problem of what my plot should be.

I think that characters make stories, and I'm drawn
to eccentricity. I had to be careful though. When
I was about half way through writing, I took a break
and read DBC Pierre's *Vernon God Little*. I thought
it was brilliant. Then I wrote two chapters with Matt
sounding distinctly Texan. They had to go. I also
read a lot of non-fiction. To get my facts straight
on the Mental Health Act and the side-effects
of medications (not to mention the evolution of
Nintendo, and various plots on *EastEnders*).

*"Characters
must lead the
way."*

**Throughout the novel, you interweave images,
letters, chapter headings and different fonts. What
is the significance of this? Do you think these
elements help in the understanding of the book?**

It is central to the novel that Matthew is physically
writing out his story, that this process takes time,
happens in different locations, and that his life is
continuing to move forwards as he writes about
it. This means that he gets distracted sometimes.
He might be sharing an event from his past when
suddenly the student social worker (the young one
with the minty breath and big gold earrings) starts
reading over his shoulder—then all he can think
about is *that*.

I'm not sure if this aids in our understanding of
the book, but I certainly think it helps us to better
understand its narrator. In the final chapter Matthew
sits at the computer for the last time, with all of his
printouts and artwork beside him.

This is how I see the piece in my mind: the crumpled
stack of Matt's writing and drawings; the typewriter
pages with their smudged ink; the letters from
Denise; the words that Patricia cut up and stuck
down with Pritt Stick. All left behind in Hope Road
Day Centre, on a table in the dark—waiting to be

found. The problem, as my publisher explained, is that this can't be stocked in bookstores. The book in your hands is our best effort at a compromise.

This novel explores mental health but it also sensitively looks at the subject of grief and how it impacts on one family. Was this something you had intended to explore in the novel, as well as the way we, as a society, handle the subject of grief?

I knew that I was going to kill Simon, so I suppose it should have been obvious. But no. I never expected grief to be such a big part of the story. I think this is a good example of how characters must lead the way.

I kill Simon Homes in chapter one, so of course there will be grieving in chapter two, perhaps a few more paragraphs of grief in three, then a meaningful flashback in chapter seven. It isn't unreasonable to plan in this way. The cast are entirely fictional; someone has to call the shots. But it doesn't work because it isn't believable. Susan Homes loses her son and her life is shattered by it. Not ruined for a couple of chapters. Shattered. There was never a time when it felt feasible to draw a line under her grief. So the grief stayed.

What would you like the reader to take away from your novel?

A desire to share it.

After completing *The Shock of the Fall*, I was interested to revisit the day of Simon's funeral. Early in the novel Matthew states:

> *I had no right to attend my brother's funeral. But I did attend. I wore a white polyester shirt that itched like mad around the collar, and a black clip-on tie. The church echoed whenever anyone coughed. And afterwards there were scones with cream and jam. And that is all I can remember.*

I considered that Matthew might remember more, bits and pieces, fragments, as the story progressed. I think including these memories would have overcrowded the novel, but I wanted to craft this section as a detached memory. The result is "All My Strength."

—Nathan Filer

——————— all of my strength ———————

'We know what you did,' he said.

'What?'

I watched his expression change, his mouth curling ever so slightly into a grin. We called him our baby cousin because he was the youngest, but he was only two weeks younger than me, and he was already taller and stronger.

His grip tightened.

'We know what you did,' he said again. 'Everyone knows.'

Then a shape moving past the window, a rattling of the garage door. Sam stiffened—and scurried away.

'I said it. I said it,' he whispered excitedly to Aaron.

And if you don't count those two, crouching on

the bottom stair, turning to watch me slam shut the bathroom door again. And if you don't count Uncle Brian, who had popped outside for a cigarette, and who I could just make out through the frosted glass— his back to the wall, one leg bent at the knee. If you don't count them, then the place to find my family was in the living room.

All huddled together, all dressed in black except for socked feet, was every relative that I had ever known. All of them. Except Simon.

And not just relatives, but friends, teachers, neighbours, everyone.

Everyone knows.

I got to staring at our toothbrushes.

Propped side-by-side in the Thorpe Park beaker. The beaker that became the toothbrush holder when Simon and me couldn't agree on which one of us it belonged to, and which one had left theirs in the car park.

I killed a bit of time doing that—running my thumb over his bristles, touching a few hundred million little bits of him. Then I thought about the funeral, but already it was crumbling away.

'Unbelievable,' Dad said.

'Is it a *horse*, Daddy?'

I couldn't remember.

'Daddy. Did you say a *horse*?'

Except I knew it wasn't a horse, because when I asked for the third time, Mum snapped, 'No. Matthew. It isn't.'

Then she might have told me what it was, but I couldn't think.

We drove in silence along the twisting roads for

a long time, the man in the black hat occasionally glancing at me in the rear view mirror. Then on the first stretch of straight road, the transit van—the van that got between our car and the-car-that-wasn't-a-horse—indicated, and pulled over.

Dad shook his head as we passed, but you could tell the driver felt bad about it. He was staring straight ahead, not wanting to look at us; the way Mum does when she cuts people up on the motorway. I felt a bit bad for him to be honest.

'It's a hearse, ami.' Dad said quietly.

Mum reached across to straighten my tie. It was a clip-on, and didn't really need straightening. I guess that was her way of saying sorry.

Here are three other things I remember from the funeral:

1.

'Wonderful, delightful,' the minister said.

He had a neatly trimmed grey beard and this soft, whispery voice that made everything he uttered sound like a secret.

'Just wonderful.'

Aunt Jacqueline raised her hands in the air, her eyes closed, singing at the top of her voice. Aunty Mel glared across the aisle at her, furious that she'd chosen this week to find God. The week when everyone else had lost something.

'Just wonderful.'

Then the silence rushed in.

The pulsing kind of silence that only happens in a big space after lots of noise.

The minister smiled at me. 'And now Simon's brother, Matthew,' he said, 'is going to share a painting.'

I stood beside him at the alter, clutching my crumpled sheet of paper. I'd painted it at Nanny Noo and Granddad's, but Nanny didn't have as many colours as we did, so for a depiction of heaven, it was pretty fucking drab.

Nobody seemed to mind though. 'And that's his N64 ... and that's his blanket ... and that's his keepsake box ... '

My voice sounded loud in the microphone.

2.

Dad did a eulogy.

That's another word I learnt.

And forgot.

He repeated the story he liked to tell us. The one with the small boy who was trying to lift a rock in his garden, and the boy's dad was watching him heave and sweat and struggle, but get nowhere. Eventually the dad asks, 'Why don't you use all of your strength?' And the boy says, 'I am, Daddy. I am using all of my strength.' And his dad says, 'No you're not. You haven't asked me for help.'

It wasn't his own story, and maybe you've heard it before. Perhaps your own dad would sit you on his knee, and sit your older brother on his other knee— whenever either of you had struggled alone.

That's what happened in our house, anyway.

Dad was sobbing into the microphone, saying how we were his strength, that we were his rock. He said he would miss Simon every day, for the rest of his life.

He looked at me when he said that, and Aunty Mel squeezed my shoulder from the row behind, and Mum squeezed my hand from next to me.

I felt squeezed.

You weren't there, I wanted to shout.

You weren't there.

Any of you.

I couldn't carry him by myself.

3.

But Dad and Uncle Brian and Uncle Paul (who wasn't really an uncle, but Dad's closest friend) and Granddad—they could carry him. Dad and Uncle Brian at the back because they were tallest, and Paul and Granddad at the front.

That's how Simon left the church, to be put back in the hearse and driven to the crematorium.

We all stood up for that bit.

A few people started clapping, but that didn't really catch on. And stuck to the heel of Uncle Brian's shoe was a small square of pink tissue paper, or probably confetti.

That's it.

That's everything.

The door handle turned.

'Are you in there?'

'Get lost, Sam.'

'It's Peter.'

Peter's my middle cousin, and if you're struggling with all of the names, don't worry because you never have to meet them. But if it helps, here's our family tree:

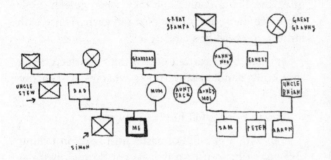

'What do you want?' I asked.

'Your mum's looking for you,' Peter said, still pressing the handle. 'She says we have to go outside. She says it's time to plant the tree.'

Ha.

'I'm coming,' I said.

It's still there. It's really tall now. If you were to drive past my parents' house today you'd see the top branches, stretching and swaying over the garage.

Aunty Mel brought it instead of flowers. CONTENTS: One sapling from our English Heritage Range; a growing-tube to protect your young tree through its first winter; and a personalized plaque, that Aunty Mel had left blank so that Mum could choose what words we wanted later, but that of course—of course, Susan—she would still like to pay for.

We took in turns to pat down the earth.

At bedtime I took Simon's toothbrush from the beaker.

I figured he wouldn't mind.

I could still hear the murmur of adult voices drifting from the living room, but they were quieter now; more like the sound of the next ten years. Those with farthest to travel had already left.

Sam had been carried out to the car asleep. Peter shook my hand because that's what we'd seen our dads do.

Simon's bristles felt funny in my mouth.

Even with a gob-full of paste, he'd keep on talking, chewing at his brush so that he got through twice as many as the rest of us.

In the long stone shower block at Ocean Cove— with the dark at the windows and the spindly daddy-longlegs and chunky moths, half flying, half stumbling against the florescent tubes—we'd stood one sink apart, brushing our teeth before bed, when this fat man wrapped in a tiny white towel took the sink between us, and started plucking the hairs in his nose.

I guess you had to be there, but it was so funny. We kept looking at each other, then looking at the man, his head tilted back, his fingers deep in his nostrils.

I can't say for sure which one of us started laughing first, but once we'd started, we couldn't stop. Simon's toothpaste froth was spitting onto the mirror—and that made us laugh even harder.

Whatever everyone knew, no-one knew that.

'Hello? Matthew? Darling?'

A

few   hundred

            million

      little

bits

      of   him.

            'Will you unlock

the door, please? Please, Matthew. I'm worried about
you.'

Time can fly when you're brushing your teeth, eh?
I mean, seriously.

It can disappear.

'What have you done?' My grandmother was
standing in the doorway. Mum's mum, the one we
call Nanny Noo. I knew it would be her. I opened
my hand, and felt a warm throbbing around the little
purple crescents.

Nanny held them to the light.

'You've broken the skin,' she said quietly.

And if you knew her, then you would know she's the
sort to keep a tube of Germolene in her handbag—
just in case. She carefully dabbed the pink paste on
with the side of her little finger, and said how she'd
always loved the smell.

I didn't know what to say, so I just said the truth.

'I held his toothbrush too tight.'

'Oh my darling. My poor darling.'

It took nothing for these grown-ups to cry.

The Cement Garden
Ian McEwan

As a schoolboy I had a determined lack of interest in reading. I would occasionally steel myself to suffer the books prescribed to us on the English syllabus, but even then if I could get away with a revision guide and the film adaptation then I would.

My journey into reading came a little later. I was a teenager when I idly plucked a copy of *The Cement Garden* from a friend's bookshelf. I was astounded by it. Still am really. Something about McEwan's precision; the control he has over each and every sentence. I found myself re-reading passages, trying to unlock their secrets. By the end I had not only discovered reading, but also knew that I wanted to write.

So Long, See You Tomorrow
William Maxwell

I was studying for a master's degree in creative writing, and well into my first draft of *The Shock of the Fall*, when my tutor recommended Maxwell's classic. He suggested I might find it helpful when thinking about my book. Detailing a tragic feud between tenant farmers in 1920s Illinois, I'll confess it wasn't immediately clear to me how they related. Then on page 27 Maxwell captures in a single perfect paragraph a notion I spend my whole novel trying to grapple. I copied it out into my notebook and referred to it often. 'In any case,' the paragraph concludes, 'in talking about the past we lie with every breath we draw.'

Catcher in the Rye
J.D. Salinger

I sometimes joke that I must owe a royalty cheque
to the Salinger estate. For all my interest in structure
and form and themes, *The Shock of the Fall* is first
and foremost a book about voice. The eccentric voice
of a socially alienated young male protagonist.

There are many, many novels in this lineage, but
I don't suppose anyone has done it better than
Salinger. I reckon Matthew and Holden Caulfield
would get along famously.

The Oxford Dictionary of Nursing
Because it's not all about fiction.
Research. Research. Research.

To Kill a Mockingbird
Harper Lee

I was tempted to bookend this list with another
British novel (I never realised how American my
reading habits have been.). But I want to mention
To Kill a Mockingbird. This was actually one of the
books that I avoided reading at school. It was on the
syllabus but I settled for the revision guide. I don't
know what made me revisit it, but I have, and very
recently. It's the book I've just finished. So I can't call
it an influence.

But you know that feeling, when you've just read
something so profoundly wonderful that you'll seize
any given opportunity to talk about it?

Well, this is me doing that.

# Reading Group Questions

1. What did you know about schizophrenia—
   either from personal experience, or as portrayed
   in popular film/television adaptations—before
   reading *The Shock of the Fall*? How, if at all,
   did this book teach you about, or change your
   impression of, this subject?

2. Discuss Matthew's relationship with his parents.
   How does it change throughout the novel?

3. Why do you think Matthew needs to tell
   his story? Is the act of writing cathartic for
   him? What about the act of *reading* about a
   character's catharsis—is it challenging? Satisfying?
   Frustrating? All of the above?

4. Discuss Matthew's portrayal of life in the
   psychiatric ward. Which descriptions were most
   meaningful—or upsetting—do you? Did this
   setting feel realistic to you as a reader? Why or
   why not?

5. Take a moment to talk about Nanny Noo. What
   are your thoughts about this character, and her
   role in the novel? w

6. In Matthew's invitation to Aaron and Jenny,
   he writes: 'I'm really sorry if I've got your name
   wrong. Part of me thinks it's Gemma. Please
   forgive me if I got it wrong. Not making excuses,
   but I am a schizophrenic.' Is this an indication
   that Matthew has come to terms with his illness?
   Why does he joke about it? How *does* the
   character—or the author—use humor to deal
   with the illness itself?

7. We are taught, as young readers, that every story
   has a 'moral'. Is there a moral to *The Shock of the
   Fall*? What can we learn about our world—and
   our selves—from Matthew's story?